LTPF
Darby, Catherine

Moon in Pisces

DATE DUE			
MR 0 8 '19			

Love is
a time of enchantment:
in it all days are fair and all fields
green. Youth is blest by it,
old age made benign:
the eyes of love see
roses blooming in December,
and sunshine through rain. Verily
is the time of true-love
a time of enchantment — and
Oh! how eager is woman
to be bewitched!

MOON IN PISCES

Lucy Bostock is only ten years old when a change of fortune snatches her from her poverty stricken London home to Ladymoon Manor in Yorkshire. In this ancient house live the Holdens, the rakish Charles and the dutiful Edward. Lucy's life becomes entangled with theirs and with the darkly handsome Saul Rowe whose family work in the mill from which the Holdens derive their wealth. In a world where Luddite riots and witchcraft march hand in hand, Lucy must pit her wits against social prejudice and danger in order to achieve her heart's desire.

Books by Catherine Darby
Published by The House of Ulverscroft:

FROST ON THE MOON

CATHERINE DARBY

MOON IN PISCES

Complete and Unabridged

ULVERSCROFT
Leicester

First published in Great Britain in 1980 by
Robert Hale Limited
London

First Large Print Edition
published 1998
by arrangement with
Robert Hale Limited
London

British Library CIP Data

Darby, Catherine, *1935* –
Moon in pisces.—Large print ed.—
Ulverscroft large print series: romance
1. Love stories
2. Large type books
I. Title
823.9'14 [F]

ISBN 0–7089–3937–6

Published by
F. A. Thorpe (Publishing) Ltd.
Anstey, Leicestershire
Set by Words & Graphics Ltd.
Anstey, Leicestershire
Printed and bound in Great Britain by
T. J. International Ltd., Padstow, Cornwall

This book is printed on acid-free paper

Prologue

1800

Her father was late again. There was nothing very unusual about that. Shelton Bostock was not a man to be relied on to be anywhere at the time he had promised. But there were lobsters for supper, bubbling away merrily in a pot on the stove and she had made a cream sauce and poured the last of the brandy into two silver tankards. They were not real silver, of course, but the brandy was excellent. Lucy knew that because she'd already taken a nip, to keep the cold out. There was only sufficient fuel for one more fire, so she had left it unlit until the last possible moment. She had however ventured to kindle the oil-lamp, and it cast a cheerful glow over the small, shabby room. The shabbiness distressed her though her father declared it was only temporary, and that when his ship came in they would move out of lodgings and buy a house of their own.

Lucy could remember dimly a time when they had lived in a house with a long, narrow garden at the back. Her mother had been

1

alive then and her father had gone out every day to his law practice in town. She could remember how gentle her mother's voice had been and how bright her eyes and cheeks. And there was a darker memory, of a tall gentleman in a silk hat and frock coat who had leaned down to look at her closely and then said, his voice grave, "This little one must be watched. In cases of consumption there is always the possibility that the disease may have been transmitted in its early stages to other members of the family."

She could remember holding her father's hand and walking with him down an avenue of dark trees to where a few people stood near a mound of earth and a hole in the ground.

After that there had been a period of confusion when she had stayed with some neighbours and her father had been away, and then he had come back and brought her to these lodgings. In the beginning they had rented two whole floors and a girl had come in every morning to clean the place, but for the past couple of years they had occupied only two rooms at the top of the house.

Shelton Bostock had gone less and less often to his office until, in the end, he had given it up altogether and touted for custom in the clubs and coffee shops, or

2

hung about the outer precincts of the Old Bailey with other indigent lawyers looking for clients. Sometimes he made money and then they were able to pay off some of the arrears of rent and buy a new dress for Lucy. There were other times when he spent the money before he got home and would return very late, his voice slurred, and a girl clinging to his arm. On those occasions Lucy would creep out and sit on the stairs with a blanket wrapped round her and try not to listen to the sounds coming from beyond the closed door.

It was hard his being late tonight because she had some particular news for him. That very morning a letter had arrived bearing a Yorkshire postmark. She had guessed that it came from her father's sister who was wed to a mill-owner up in the north. Lucy had never met Aunt Trinity Holden, but her father mentioned her occasionally.

"She was a pretty girl. Fair hair and grey eyes, always smiling. She married a man called Matthew Holden. I was away at school at the time but he seemed a decent enough fellow. My twin-brother, Richmond was alive then."

Richmond had gone to sea and been killed in the French wars. Lucy couldn't remember him at all though her father said he'd visited them once when she was a small baby.

Aunt Trinity Holden had never been down to London. "Not that there's ever been an open quarrel," Shelton had explained. "Father married a Scotswoman and emigrated to America just after the Forty Five. Trinity and Richmond and I were born there, and after my mother died, we were reared by my Father's half-sister, Tamar Makin. After he died she brought us back to this country. I was about fourteen then. We were sent off to school, to get us out of the way, I suspect. Aunt Tamar never had much patience with boys. In her Will she left everything to Trinity. Richmond and I were left to make our own way as well as we could. Trinity married Matthew Holden and settled down at Ladymoon Manor."

Ladymoon Manor. For some reason the name fascinated Lucy. She rolled the two words around her tongue, wondering what the house would be like and if she would ever see it. Although there had been no open breach her father had drifted away from his family and apart from an occasional letter, there had been no contact since. And her mother, Jane Ashcroft, had been an orphan, a clergyman's daughter with only a tiny annuity of her own.

The letter was propped up on the

4

mantleshelf, its sloping handwriting very elegant and sharp. She kept glancing up at it from where she sat at the window. The clock told her it was already past ten, and the narrow street was quite dark, fog rolling in from the river to intensify the March gloom.

"He will be home soon," she said aloud.

She had moved the pan of lobsters away from the little charcoal stove, and the supper was cooling rapidly. If he didn't come soon the whole meal would be spoiled. Lucy bit her lip in vexation and peered again through the window. Surely he would come home soon. Surely he had not forgotten that it was her birthday!

Only the previous day he had chucked her under the chin and said jovially, "Ten years old tomorrow, my Pisces girl! And I tell you in confidence, my sweet, that my ship is nearly in harbour."

"Have you been given a case?," she asked eagerly.

"Not exactly *given* one," he returned, "but I have the promise, the firm promise, of a most interesting legal tangle to be sorted out. With great profits for all concerned. Think of that, Lucy!"

"We can get the gold watch and my seed pearls out of pawn," Lucy said.

It was too bad of him not to have come home. She had even put on her best dress of pale yellow muslin with little, puffed sleeves and a high waist, and had curled her hair into a frizz of tight red ringlets. It was a great pity she had inherited her father's red hair and narrow face. Nobody could ever call her a pretty child. Her mouth was too big and she had freckles on her nose.

There were footsteps on the stairs. She sprang up, her head raised eagerly. The footsteps were heavy, heavier than her father's. She went over to the door and opened it cautiously.

A tall shape, broader than her father's shape, blocked the narrow landing. Lucy stared up at him, her brow wrinkling in puzzlement.

"Are you any relation to Shelton Bostock?" a deep voice enquired.

"I'm Lucy, his daughter," she said.

"Is your mother at home?"

"My mother's dead, sir. I'm waiting for my father."

"You won't mind if I step inside? My name's Hallet — Jim Hallet."

In the lamplight she could see him more clearly. Youngish, heavy side whiskers, small bright eyes.

"You're a constable, sir," she said.

6

"That's right. You're a sharp one, and no mistake!" His eyes roved across the room and settled on the glowing stove. "That smells good," he commented.

"It's lobster, sir."

"And a cream sauce to go with it. That's a brave supper for a hungry man."

"Would you — we could spare some for you," she said politely.

"Now that's a handsome invitation," he said genially. "Shall we have a bite together? And I'll set a light to the fire. It's a mite chilly up here and that dress of yours is very thin. Have you no shawl to wrap round yourself?"

"Yes, sir." She took it from the back of the door and knotted it round her shoulders.

The fire crackled into life. The constable handed down two plates and began to slice bread. Lucy loaded sauce over the lobster in silence. A nameless dread was growing in her but if she went on doing small, unimportant tasks she might stave off the knowledge of it.

"Now this is cosy!" he exclaimed, seating himself and waving her to the other side of the table. "You'll not object if I sup up the juice with my bread? 'Tis a shame to waste a drop of such flavour!"

"My father — " Lucy began and stopped,

7

frowning down at her plate.

"Yes, my duckling." He spoke gravely, answering the question she had not asked.

She ate in silence for a minute or two, chewing daintily.

"He was taken ill at a gentleman's club," Constable Hallet said. "There was a doctor there and he did everything possible, but it was a heart attack. He lived only a few minutes."

"I see." She felt numb, as if the news referred to someone else.

"Have you any other family, my duckling?" he asked.

"An aunt," she said slowly, trying to pierce through the fog of unreality. "There's a letter — I suppose it will be all right to open it now."

"It might be best," he agreed.

The letter unsealed, she frowned at it doubtfully.

"Would you like me to read it while you get on with your supper?" he asked.

"If you don't mind, sir. I don't — my reading's not so good," she said awkwardly.

"Let's see what's here then." He smoothed out the creased paper and read aloud.

"Ladymoon Manor, near York."

"That's the address," Lucy interrupted. "It's a big house on the moors."

"It begins, 'My dear Shelton. It is now some years since we were last in touch, though I have often thought about you and wondered how you and Lucy were faring, and even if you were still at the address you sent to us when your wife died.'"

"That was my mother. Her name was Jane."

"And I'm sure she was a very lovely woman. Now, where was I? Ah, yes. 'I have felt for some time that we ought to meet again. Would it be possible for you and Lucy to pay us a long visit? Country air would surely benefit the little girl and the moors look very beautiful in springtime, as you must remember. Matthew joins with me in this invitation. Your affectionate sister, Trinity Holden.'"

"She sounds very kind," Lucy said.

"You don't know her?"

"No, sir. We never went up to Yorkshire at all, but she has written once or twice before."

"She would give you a home, I imagine?"

"I'm sure she would, but I don't see why I can't stay here."

"Oh, but I think you can see," he said. "Little girls cannot live all alone. The streets are full of beggars, and I would not like to see you among them. It will be better for you to go to Yorkshire."

"What shall I do then?" she asked in a small voice.

"Finish your supper and drink down the brandy," he advised. "Is there anyone who can stay with you tonight? The landlady?"

"I don't want anybody," she said.

"There was money in your father's wallet," Constable Hallet said. "He'd won something earlier at the tables. Seven guineas."

She stared at the little heap of coin, her throat closing up against a sob.

"I could come back in the morning," he offered, "and see that you got on the stagecoach. You'd be in York in three or four days time, and you could get transport on to your aunt's. I'll put you in charge of the driver, so he'll see you get there."

"What about?" She hesitated.

"I can arrange for your father to be decently buried, everything very tasteful and done in a gentlemanly fashion. Where does your mother lie?"

"In — Highgate Cemetery, I think."

"Then it'll be in the registers. They can probably be laid together. I can arrange all nicely for you. Your father's been formally identified by his companions and was laid out in a back room. You'll not need to upset yourself by seeing him."

She was filled with an aching hunger to see him just once more, but she nodded and said, "Thank you kindly."

"Five of these will pay for the burying and buy you a seat on the stage coach," Constable Hallet said, sorting the coins. "That leaves two guineas for your own needs."

"There's the rent to be paid up," she remembered.

"I'll have a word with the landlord in the morning. He'll likely agree to take the furniture, if it belongs to you."

"He can have it all," she said, "except the clock. It was my mother's clock."

"And a very pretty one," he approved.

"It has two fish at each side of the clock face," she said proudly. "My mother was born in March, you see, and that makes her Pisces. She was interested in things like that."

"Was she now? She must have been a very clever lady," he said. "I think she'd have been very proud of such a brave daughter. Now I'll stir up the fire for you and be on my way. You'll not be afraid here by yourself?"

"No, sir. I'm accustomed to being alone."

"Lock the door after me then. I'll be here in the morning, so you'll be packed and ready, will you?"

"Yes, sir." She opened the door for him and bobbed a curtsey as he went out.

The room was warm now and fog muffled any discordant notes from the street below. Lucy went and sat down again at the table. After a moment she began to finish up her supper, chewing it very carefully and forcing it past the lump in her throat.

Four days later, a green shawl covering her muslin dress and a small green bonnet tied on her curly head, Lucy sat bolt upright in a small pony trap as it rattled and swayed across the moors.

Everything had happened so quickly that she still felt confused when she tried to sort out events in her own mind. The landlord had accepted the furniture in lieu of the rent, and Constable Hallet had given her a letter for Aunt Trinity and taken her to the stage where he had settled her at an inside window seat, with a bag of sugar plums, and told the driver that particular care was to be taken of her.

The journey had been unlike anything she had ever known in her life. By the end of the first day her bones felt as if they were about to break after the jolting of the coach, and there was a red mark across her palm where she had clung to the window-strap.

The other passengers had been very kind,

pointing out landmarks of interest on the road, offering her sips of lemonade from their own refreshments, and at the posting inns she had been given a good meal and a little room to herself.

Constable Hallet had obviously told the driver something of her circumstances, for he kept on shaking his head sadly whenever he caught sight of her at the halting places, and lifting her down to the ground with a rumbling, "There, little miss! Now we'll get you fed and bedded!"

The miles stretched behind and ahead of her, the landscape constantly changing from town to countryside and back again. As they travelled further northward one or two of the passengers began to murmur among themselves about the possibility of footpads and highwaymen. The prospect of being held up struck Lucy as more of an excitement than anything else, but the gentlemen travelling with her had loosened pistols in their holsters and one plump female was heard to declare that if any footpad tried to lay hands on her virtue she would run him through with her parasol.

They had rattled into York however, without having met a single highwayman, and Lucy had been squeezed into a corner at a round table on which boiled beef and

13

ale was set out for her, while the driver of the stagecoach had entered into an animated but inaudible conversation with a thick-set fellow in labouring garb, at the conclusion of which the latter had come over to where Lucy sat, eyed her narrowly and said, "You'll be wanting to go out to Ladymoon Manor, they say."

"If you please, sir."

"No need to call me sir," the man said. "Elisha Rowe is my name, and I work for Master Holden. I'm on my way back to Ladymoon now, so you can come along with me, if you've finished your meal."

"I'm ready now," she said, swallowing the rest of her bitter ale and standing up.

"Is this all your baggage?" he demanded, lifting the small, rather battered trunk at her feet.

"Yes, sir — Elisha."

"Come on then, I'm behind as it is. Saul!"

Emerging into the cobbled yard Elisha raised his voice in a shout. A boy, taller and a couple of years older than Lucy, ducked around the corner and seized the reins of a sturdy pony standing between the shafts of a small trap.

"Get up behind," Elisha ordered, giving the boy a quick clip across the head. "A

14

few hours off from the mill and you sneak off the minute my back's turned."

"Who's the lass?" the boy demanded, staring at her.

"Name of Lucy Bostock. She's kin to Mistress Holden. Not that it's any of my business, so climb up and look sharp."

Elisha gave the boy a poke and turned to lift Lucy up to the high seat. She clung there, feeling suddenly deserted, for the stage-coach driver had not even troubled to say goodbye.

"Is it far?" she ventured.

"Three or four hours. It'll be dusk when we get there."

From the back of the trap the boy raised his voice. "It's cold so tha's better wrap warm, little lass."

"Hold thy clack!" the other said brusquely. "And she's Miss Lucy to us."

Lucy would have liked to go on talking to the boy, but his father — she supposed it was his father — cracked his whip over the pony's back and sent the animal jerking forward over the cobbles.

At least she was in the fresh air after the stuffiness of the coach. The wind was sharp, but neither man nor boy seemed to notice it. Elisha drove steadily out onto a wide track that curved and dipped over steep meadows

15

of short, wiry grass. There were sheep dotted about, many with lambs frisking about them, and several times Lucy glimpsed the scut of a rabbit as it bounded for cover into the longer grass.

Once she saw high walls away to the right and said eagerly, "Is that Ladymoon Manor?"

"That's Holden Hall," Elisha said.

"Holden? Does it belong to my uncle then?"

"Used to be in his family but Master Lumley owns it now," he told her. "Lives there with his daughter."

"How old is she?"

Elisha shrugged but Saul spoke up from the back of the trap.

"Sarah's fifteen. Her dad's got black blood, miss. Real black blood."

"Good heavens!" Lucy said politely.

Elisha snorted. "What Saul means," he said, "is that Master Lumley's mam or dad was black African, but Master Lumley would pass for a Spaniard, I reckon. They do say he came over here in a slaver, but he's a free man now and a rich one. Married a girl from Otley and she left him a daughter."

"My aunt has two sons," Lucy remembered.

"Master Charles and Master Edward,"

Elisha nodded. "You'll be meeting them both."

"That's our house!" Saul cried, waving his arm towards a grey stone building set in a neat garden. "We live there."

"We?"

"I've six," Elisha said. "Saul here's the eldest. Seems my wife cannot leave off breeding."

"Do you — you said you worked for my uncle."

"Overseer, and ought to be at the mill now, but I'd business over in York."

"I'm going to be overseer when I'm grown," Saul announced.

"Then tha' mun frame thysen to work," his father said, lapsing into the thick, drawling accent that Lucy found so difficult to follow.

"Where is the mill?" she asked.

"Down along the river. You cannot see it from here."

"Oh." She would have liked to ask more questions but he had lapsed into silence, so she contented herself with looking about her as they drove on.

Dusk was settling down over the horizon, draining colour from the grass. Here and there a thin plume of smoke rose from the chimney of a cottage. In the fading light she could see a huddle of buildings ahead.

"We're here," Elisha said briefly. They were approaching what was evidently the back of the estate. Lucy picked out a couple of barns and what looked like stables at a little distance from the main building. Elisha drew up in a small paved yard and raised his voice again in a shout.

A door opened and a girl of about her own age propelled herself through it.

"Emma, this is Miss Lucy. You'd best take her through to the master," Elisha ordered.

"Whatever are you doing back here? Did Ainsworth not receive my message?"

A tall man, grey hair silvered by the light from the passage behind him, shouldered the girl aside.

"Master Ainsworth said he'd give the price you wanted for the ewes," Elisha said.

"Then be off home. Who is this you have with you?"

"'Tis your wife's niece, sir. She was waiting in York."

"My wife's niece!" The man came to the side of the trap and stared at her. "Are you Shelton's girl?"

"Yes, sir. I'm Lucy," she said timidly.

"And where's your father? Trinity sent invitation for both."

"He's dead, sir, so I came alone," she said simply.

18

"All by yourself up from London?" he said incredulously.

"In charge of the stagecoach driver, sir," Elisha volunteered. "She was in the taproom of the Horse and Crown, waiting for transport."

"And as it was a fortunate chance that you brought her, I'll not enquire what took you to the Horse and Crown in the first place," the other said wryly. "Charles! Charles, come over here and see what's landed on the doorstep! Your Uncle Shelton's girl, if you please!"

Another tall figure emerged from the open door and came to the side of the trap.

"Is this Cousin Lucy?" the newcomer said.

"So she claims. She has her father's looks."

"He was obviously no beauty then," Charles said. "What a bag of bones the child is!"

"I have a letter from Constable Hallet," Lucy said.

"We'd best go inside," her uncle decided. "Is this your bag?"

"Yes, sir. I can manage it."

Lifted to the ground, she clutched the handle of the battered little trunk.

"I'll go and tell mother," Charles said, vanishing again.

"You'd best be off home," the older man said, nodding and frowning at Elisha. "Tell your Saul to keep a still tongue until we get to the truth of this. Emma, go and put a warming pan in the blue room, and ask Cook to make some soup or something. The child will need to feed and sleep."

With Lucy at his heels he strode back into the passage. It led into a dairy and thence through a wide corridor stacked with jars of pickle and preserves into an enormous kitchen. There was a fire roaring in the biggest hearth Lucy had ever seen and two girls washing dishes at a stone sink. At the further end of the room a raised and curtained platform revealed a glimpse of a table laid with the remains of a meal.

They crossed a narrow hall and came into a square, panelled parlour where another fire burned brightly. Charles was on the arm of a high-backed chair talking earnestly to a lady who sat there. At a little distance a younger man in the sombre garb of a curate was listening intently.

Three pairs of eyes swivelled to inspect her. She stood, holding onto the trunk, uncomfortably aware that her bonnet was slightly crooked and the tip of her nose pink with cold.

"Is this true, Matthew?" The lady's greying hair still had gleams of gold and her grey eyes were long-lashed. "Is this really Shelton's little girl?"

"She says she has a letter," Matthew Holden said.

"It's here, sir." Lucy put down the trunk and fumbled in the drawstring bag at her waist. "The constable wrote it for me, and there's a paper with it to say my father is dead."

"Sit down while I get to the bottom of this," Matthew said.

Handing the documents to him, Lucy sat down obediently on a low, embroidered stool. It was, she thought, a most elegant apartment with a silver candelabrum holding numerous tapers and a small harpsichord in the corner. Thin, muted rugs covered the polished floor and a cabinet against the wall held an array of crystal.

"The letter is explicit," Matthew said, handing it to his wife. "It seems that Shelton died suddenly at the end of last week and this is his girl."

"But he enjoyed such good health," Trinity said, "I cannot understand what can have happened."

"The death certificate certifies a heart attack," Charles pointed out.

21

"But the funeral? Who saw to that?" she said anxiously.

"He's been buried with my mother, in Highgate Cemetery," Lucy said.

They looked at her in faint surprise as if they had forgotten she was there. Then Matthew, taking the seat opposite his wife, said, "This Constable Hallet seems to have acted very properly, indeed to have exceeded his duty. He has arranged everything and, I suspect, has dipped into his own pocket in order to do so. Five guineas cannot possibly have covered all the expenses."

"We ought to have done more for Shelton," Trinity said. "After his wife died — "

"You know very well that he would have nothing from us," her husband said. "Shelton and Richmond always went their own way."

"And now both are gone." Tears came into the fine grey eyes and trembled on the edges of the long lashes. "Richmond killed in action at sea and Shelton died in what I can only describe as penury! It is too sad to contemplate."

"Then don't contemplate it," Charles said. "Wipe your eyes and cheer up, mother. You will do no good by upsetting yourself."

"We ought to be thinking of the child," said the younger man. "She must be very tired and confused after such a long journey."

22

"Dear Edward! You always see things so clearly!" Trinity said.

"I told Emma to air the blue room and to get cook to make some soup." Matthew said.

"That was thoughtful of you, my dear." Trinity turned to Lucy and gazed at her. "Take off your bonnet and shawl," she invited. "You are very like your father. We never met your mother but Shelton wrote to tell us how happy they were together, and we were sorry to hear of her death."

"I don't believe even Shelton had hair of such startling shade," Matthew said critically.

"And her eyes are as green as a cat," Charles observed. "It's a mercy you didn't put her up in the red room, father. She'd have clashed dreadfully with the wallpaper!"

"Here is Emma with the soup. Draw up a table, Edward, and pass a napkin. She can eat it here, and perhaps some apple tart to follow. Do you like apple tart, my dear?"

"Just soup, if you please," Lucy said. As she spooned up the thick, meaty stew, Lucy heard the talk break out again over her head.

"A polite little thing! You always wanted a daughter, mother."

"To think of her being all alone in lodgings, poor child. We should have insisted on her

23

being sent to us when her mother died."

"Well, we have her now, my dear and not, I fear, with many worldly goods. Your brothers were most improvident, I fear."

"Have you been to school, Lucy?"

This was from Edward who had dropped to one knee at her side. His face was plainer and gentler than his brother's, his voice kind.

"I went sometimes to a dame school," she said shyly. "We did reading and writing and counting on a bead frame there, and there was a globe of the world with the sea marked in blue. Then the teacher was sick and when she was better she moved away and the school closed down."

"But what did you do with yourself all day?" he persisted.

"I kept the house clean," she said, sensing criticism, "and I went early to the markets. Food is cheaper then, and you can pick up a nice bit of fish or a pile of greens for next to nothing. And sometimes we'd go out on the river in a boat or over to Chelsea for a spot of tea."

"Did your father never take you to church?"

"Once or twice," she said, trying to remember. "There were flowers on the altar and boys singing about the resurrect — resurrection. It was interesting, but father

24

snored very loud, and the next time I wanted to go we couldn't because his good boots were in pawn and he was short of the ready."

"The ready what?" Trinity asked.

Charles gave a shout of laughter. "Money, my dear mother," he said. "Uncle Shelton did not, I fear, believe in protecting his offspring from the realities of life. She is probably accustomed to roaming the seamier districts of London all day and half the night."

"I did not." Roused to indignation Lucy clattered her spoon into the bowl. "Most nights I was in bed by ten, except when Father brought back a doxy!"

"The child's a complete heathen," Edward said. "We cannot allow this state of affairs to go on. It is our responsibility — "

"Pray don't begin to lecture us on our responsibilities," Charles yawned. "You used to be quite agreeable, Edward, until you became a clergyman and caught religion."

"Don't quarrel, boys," their father said, indulgently as if they were much younger than their years. "Trinity, my dear, the decision is yours. Shelton was your brother and this is his child after all."

"I could make shift to teach her, I suppose," her aunt said doubtfully.

"Mother, you haven't opened a book in

25

years!" Edward said. "In fact it wouldn't surprise me if you hadn't forgotten how to read!"

"I could spare a couple of hours myself each morning," Matthew said. "With Charles spending more time at the counting house I can afford to indulge myself a little."

"In teaching? I never knew you were interested in teaching," Trinity said, looking amused.

"I can teach her sufficient for a female to know," he said. "You can teach her something of music and drawing, my dear. Charles can give her riding instructions and Edward will, no doubt, bestir himself in the matter of her religious upbringing. Between us we may bring her up to something more than a heathen."

"You'll never bring her up to be a beauty," Charles said. "She's a scrawny piece if ever I saw one."

"She may turn out to be quite striking," Trinity said kindly. "Certainly we'll have to furnish her with a more suitable wardrobe. Muslin in March, if you please!"

"It's my best dress," Lucy said.

"And not suitable for a little girl," Trinity said firmly. "I think too that you will want to wear more sober colours for a few months out of respect for your father. I shall go into

26

black myself for a month. Edward, you ought to go down to London to make certain that everything has been done properly for my poor brother."

"I can go down next month if that suits you," he returned. "After that, if I get the new living at Clutterhouses, my time will be fully occupied."

"You are certain to get the living. It is in Daniel Lumley's gift," Trinity said.

"I fail to understand why my brother's ambitions should be tied to the whim of a man like Lumley," Charles began.

"Let us not rake up that old argument again," Matthew interrupted. "We have more than enough to satisfy our needs without coveting our neighbour's goods as well."

"Certainly more than Shelton ever had," Trinity said, rising gracefully.

Her loose gown of silvery velvet flowed gracefully about her. She was a pretty woman, a trifle plump for current tastes, but with a charming smile. Lucy had already noticed that her eyes turned constantly to her husband and that whenever he spoke she listened with almost rapt attention.

"We will have prayers now, and then Lucy must go up to bed," she said. "The poor child must be exhausted after so many days travelling."

They went back into the narrow hall and into a small room at the back. Like the parlour this apartment was also panelled in dark oak, but its floor was tiled in a mosaic of golden stars and blue flowers, and its high window was round and uncurtained. There were a few chairs placed in a semicircle, shelves of books down one wall, a small fire burning in an elaborately carved hearth. Lucy's eyes flew at once to a low table beneath the high window on which stood a gleaming cup. Flanked by candles it stood proudly, its golden surface sparkling in the mellow light. At each side of the bowl snakes with silver tongues twined themselves into handles. On the cup itself, traced in silver, a woman's smiling face gazed, slant-eyed, the head surmounted by a crescent moon.

"That is a very old and valuable cup," Matthew said, noting Lucy's interest. "It has been in this house for centuries. Even before this present house was built in the sixteenth century the cup was hidden here under the tiles. There was a Roman villa here once, nearly a thousand years ago. Can you imagine, my dear, that all those many years ago people actually lived here and used the cup?"

"It's my belief that it is a very early

communion cup," Edward put in. "Certainly it's very beautiful."

Lucy sat down on one of the chairs and gazed at the cup. It seemed, she thought, to draw all the light into itself and to quiver as if it burst with a life of its own. A strange, secret life older than anything any of them could imagine.

The little room was filling up now, the servants coming in to kneel on leather pads. Lucy twisted round in her chair to count them. Three very young girls in mob caps and long white pinafores, a plump woman who was obviously the cook, a bow-legged man with heavy side whiskers and two younger men who tugged at their forelocks and grinned at her.

"Sit still, child," Trinity whispered from her own chair. "'Tis bad manners to fidget."

Lucy sat still, fixing a brightly interested look on her face. Edward moved to the table and swept a commanding glance around his small congregation. There was a certain dignity about him that impressed her. It was as if he had come into his own sphere, and his voice, when he spoke. was resonant.

"We gather here tonight to offer thanks for the fruits of our labour today. Let us praise the Lord for them. I would also ask you to pray for the soul of my uncle, Shelton

Bostock, who passed away four days since. I did not know him personally but I am hopeful he died in the mercy of the Lord. And we are very pleased, in the midst of our sorrow, to welcome into our midst his daughter, Lucy. She is now a member of the household and we greet her with affection."

He paused to smile at her, but Lucy's green eyes were riveted on the golden cup. The face on it was the face she had known once in a dream she could not remember. An ancient face that never grew old, veiled sometimes in blue mist, at other times so clear that its beauty caught at her heart like anguish.

The walls about her expanded, the dark panels fading into white marble that soared like wings up into a dome so high that she could not even see it by tilting her head. Fine white sand squeezed between her bare toes, and drifted beneath the pylon gate. A dog-headed god and a cow-headed goddess watched her as she moved across the black and white floor, her small feet tapping the cool stone of alternating squares.

Men with shaven heads in leopard skins, girls in white robes with cones of perfumed wax on their heads and thick, fringed wigs of black hair. A lion cub chained to the foot of a massive pillar, flicking its tail idly, narrowing amber eyes as she went past into the spiralling incense that rose about the towering throne on which the veiled figure sat. Blue wings folded, long fingers clasped about a lotus flower, eyes long and secret lips parted in the hint of a smile.

"Who are you, Lady? Tell me your name?"

Lips parting further, the petals of the lotus trembling, a soft sighing of wind.

"For Thine is the Kingdom, the Power and the Glory. Amen," said Edward Holden. "Mother, you'd best take Lucy to bed. The poor child is nearly asleep."

"Come along, my dear," Trinity said promptly. "We can pick up your trunk as we go back through the parlour. Would you like to go to the closet before we go up? It's just outside the kitchen door."

"If you please, mistress."

"You must call me Aunt Trinity," the other said smilingly. "Go along now and I'll wait for you here."

The servants stared at her with undisguised curiosity as she went through the kitchen.

It was cooler in the passage beyond, so cool that she shivered in her thin dress. Returning she was confronted by the girl who had first met the trap, and whose name was Emma.

"I've put the warming pan in the blue bed," the girl said.

"Thank you," Lucy stood awkwardly, aware that the other servants had lowered their own voices in an effort to listen.

"I'm Emma, miss. It was my dad brought you," the girl said.

"Then Saul is your brother. He seems — a very pleasant boy."

"He'll do, as brothers go. There's two younger at home and the babies."

"Do you live here?"

"I sleep in the loft with Nell and Jessie. Cook has a room to herself back of the dairy and the lads sleep over the stables."

"And that's enough gossip. Let the little one go her way," one of the older maids said.

"If you need anything," Emma said, her dark eyes brightly friendly, "call on me. Anytime."

"Are you comfortable now, dear?" Trinity asked as Lucy came into the hall again.

"I was talking to Emma," Lucy said, glancing at the door of the room where they had said prayers. It was closed now, the gleaming cup hidden from view,

"Emma Rowe? The Rowes have worked at Ladymoon for generations." Trinity said. "One of Elisha's aunts was housekeeper here

32

when I was a girl. Three of his sons work in the mill, and we took Emma a year back as a maid. She's a good girl, but apt to be forward. The gentlemen are in the library, so come and make your goodnights."

They had walked through the parlour, across a wider hall out of which stairs reached up to a broad, shallow landing, and now reached double doors at which Trinity rapped sharply before entering.

The three men were in attitudes of ease, stretched in leather chairs with glasses of madeira in their hands. It was a large, high-ceilinged apartment, its furniture solidly masculine, guns and pistols ranged in a glass case, books filling one wall.

"I'm taking Lucy up to bed now," Trinity said.

Seen together the three of them bore a marked family resemblance, their hair fair, their eyes blue. But there were differences. Matthew was greying and heavy-shouldered, Edward gentler without Charles's darting quickness. She was a little afraid of Charles.

"Good-night." She spoke shyly, bobbing a curtsey, her green eyes lowered.

"Don't forget to say your prayers," Edward cautioned.

She lugged the trunk across the hall again and up to where the stairs divided to left and right, and twisted round again into a narrow flight.

"Your uncle and I sleep there," Trinity said, indicating a door on the left. "The two little rooms on the right are used as sewing-room and winter parlour now. There are two guest rooms up there, but from now on the blue room will be yours. Your cousins have rooms at the far end of the corridor. Here we are then! You'll be comfortable here?"

Puffing slightly, she set down the lamp she was carrying and went to pull the blue curtains across the windows.

"You can see the mill chimney at the bend in the river from here." she said. "The garden stretches to the bank and below is the river. We can go down there tomorrow for a walk if you like. I'll send Emma up with hot water. There's warm water in the jug now, so you can sponge your hands and face. Shall I help you to unpack."

Lucy shook her head. The room, with its blue carpet and hangings and four-poster bed, looked immense. In the long mirror she was very small and thin, the yellow dress unsuitable for a child.

At the door her aunt said in a breathless little rush of words.

"I do hope you will be happy with us, my

34

dear. It is quite a long time since there was a child in the house, but we will make out very well, I'm sure."

She went out and Lucy was alone in the big blue room. She knelt down and unhasped the straps of the trunk. Her two woollen gowns, a clean shift, stockings and slippers were folded around the clock. She lifted it out, wound it carefully, and put it on the dressing-table. It looked very small, even smaller than she was herself. Aloud she said, her voice trembling. "That's a very sad little clock, you know. A very sad little clock."

Part One

1

1809

Lucy Bostock stood in front of the long glass in her bedroom and studied her reflection critically. It was her nineteenth birthday but any hope she had ever had of turning into a beauty overnight had long since evaporated. Nevertheless she did think that her appearance was pleasing. Her high-waisted coat dress of corn yellow satin had a high collar and a shoulder cape fastened with narrow tassels of dark fur. Her poke-bonnet of yellow satin was edged with the same fur. The colour and style suited her slim figure and creamy complexion, the wide brim of her bonnet revealed only a few straying locks of curly red hair. It was a pity her mouth was still so wide and her eyes so green, but she had sound teeth and a low, husky voice that trembled often on the edge of laughter.

It was unlikely that anyone would have remembered her birthday. In the two years since her uncle's death, Aunt Trinity had lapsed into a kind of gentle dream. It was as if, with the death of her husband, her

39

real life had ceased and she had begun to withdraw from reality, to bury herself in pleasant memories of a life that had been harmonious and unchanging.

"Though I have had sad times, my dear," she had told Lucy. "Life was very hard when I was a young girl living in America. I was very glad when I was married to your uncle and we settled down comfortably together. There was no mill here then, but Matthew built one with money his own father left to him. And it has provided employment for nearly everyone in the area. That gives me very great satisfaction."

One could see the high chimney of Holden Mill from the upper windows of the manor, but the river that flowed past the front garden was unchanged. It was a beautiful river, not wide but winding between banks of meadowsweet and tall grasses heavy with violets. Among the trailing brambles were arches and bits of wall of the same grey stone as the manor.

"For the house was built long ago from the ruins of a nunnery that used to stand down by the river," Aunt Trinity had said. "A long time ago that was, of course, and now there's only a few stones left. Sad really to think about it!"

Lucy had not thought it very sad at all. She

had never visited a nunnery in her life, but she thought they were probably very gloomy places. It was, in her opinion, much more sensible to build a beautiful manor-house where people could live happily.

The two rooms where she had lived with her father were now no more than vague pictures in her memory. She had sunk her roots so deeply into Ladymoon Manor that it was a surprise when she remembered that she had not actually been born there, for she could not imagine ever having lived anywhere else. The little girl who had clutched her battered trunk so tightly had become no more than another cloudy picture in her mind. The reality was this slim, elegantly attired young lady who appraised her reflection and was not ill-pleased with what she saw.

Humming under her breath she ran down the twisting stairs into the parlour where Aunt Trinity sat by the fire. The older woman's smile was as sweet but rolls of fat had coarsened her graceful figure. Though she ate little at table she was continually nibbling at bonbons, and it was months since she had even walked to the bottom of the garden.

She looked up as Lucy came in, blinked still beautiful grey eyes and said, "Not rushing off somewhere, are you? Emma says the wind is quite sharp."

"Only over to Holden Hollow. I've some things for the Rowes."

"There isn't sickness in the family, is there?"

"Annie has the croup. I promised to take some blackcurrant cordial, and a pot of honey."

"Very kind, my dear. Your uncle would have approved," Trinity said vaguely.

"Was there anything you wanted, aunt?"

"Anything I wanted? No, I don't think — heavens, but there is! It quite slipped my mind."

"What slipped your mind?"

"An invitation from Daniel Lumley. His daughter is coming home this week and he proposes to give a supper party for her. A few neighbours and friends he says."

"He never gave a party before," Lucy commented, turning the invitation over in her hands.

"I suspect that after four years in London Sarah wishes to impress us all with her brilliant sophistication," Trinity said.

"She never did anything when we met but bow and smile," Lucy said. "I don't believe I've heard her speak more than half a dozen sentences."

"She was shy, I suppose. It cannot have

been very exciting living in that great barn of a house with only her father for company. It was probably the best course of action that Daniel Lumley could have taken."

"Charles says he was hoping to catch a husband for her, but as he won't consider anything lower than a duke, his bid failed."

"You must not take what Charles says too seriously," Trinity said. "Charles has always felt that Holden Hall should have remained in the family, but neither Matthew nor I ever liked the place. But we have never been on intimate visiting terms with the Lumleys."

"I hope he will agree to take us to the party," Lucy said.

"Charles and Edward can escort you, my dear," Trinity said. "But you must make my excuses. I am far too old to be jolted over the moors in an uncomfortable carriage for the purpose of spending several hours in a house I dislike with people I hardly ever see. But if you are going anywhere near the mill you could take the invitation over to Charles. He will wish to send an answer."

"Was there anything else you wanted?" Lucy put the giltedged card into her reticule.

"I don't think so, dear." Trinity selected an almond from the silver dish at her side.

43

"You were not thinking of walking down to Holden Hollow?"

"I shall take the trap." Lucy kissed her aunt on the cheek and escaped before she was drawn into an argument on the dangers of driving about all by herself.

The garden was spattered with sunshine. She stood for a moment, looking up at the ivy covered facade of the house. With its diamond paned windows and solid oak door, it never failed to give her pleasure. When she had first heard of Sarah Lumley's going to London she had felt, not envy, but a vague sense of wonder that anyone could bear to go into the city when it was possible to remain in the countryside. She had never felt the faintest desire to return to the grimy streets, or even to visit the cemetery where her parents lay.

In the yard the pony was already hitched to the trap and Emma was putting in the covered blanket. At twenty Emma Rowe was a bold eyed girl with a magnificent figure. It was rumoured that she allowed the village lads certain liberties, but she was demure enough as she went about her household duties. She looked up now as Lucy settled herself in the driving seat and said, "It'll rain later, miss, if you're thinking of your new bonnet."

"I think it'll hold off. Do you have any message for your mother? I'm going down to the Hollow."

"Tell her I'll be over on Sunday afternoon — if that's all right with you, miss?"

"You had last Sunday afternoon off," Lucy said doubtfully.

"To help out with our Annie, miss. Mother's in the family way again and she's not fit to cope with Annie being so frail."

"I didn't know." Lucy took up the reigns and nodded pleasantly. "I'll speak to my aunt but I'm sure she'll let you take the afternoon off again."

"Thank you, miss." The bold, dark eyes flicked down in gratitude as Emma stepped back.

Lucy took the curving track that led away from the stables, then branched off towards the mill.

A straggle of small cottages dipped into the valley. The millworkers lived here, paying only token rent. Matthew Holden had kept the cottages in good repair but in the two years since his death Charles had taken little interest in their upkeep. Driving past, Lucy noticed slates missing from two or three roofs and several panes of cracked and broken glass in the windows. Behind each cottage a strip of land had been fenced off for the growing

45

of vegetables but most of them were weed-ridden and overgrown, the fences sagging, paint peeling from the gates.

The Rowe house stood apart from the rest on higher ground. Stone built with six rooms, it boasted a kitchen garden and a grove of fruit trees. But this garden too was neglected, the house in need of paint and repairs. She hitched up the trap and went briskly up to the door. It was half open and from the room beyond came the sound of a thin, fretful wailing.

"Is that you, Elisha?" A woman's voice, half-hopeful, half-fearful, reached her as she stepped inside.

"Mrs Rowe? It's only me." Lucy set the basket on the table and looked round at the dusty floor, the uncleared hearth.

"Oh, it's you, Miss Lucy."

Anna Rowe, a child hiccupping in her arms, another swelling out the front of her dress, came from an inner room. "I thought it was Elisha."

"Isn't he at the mill?"

Anna shook her head, raising her hand to smooth back the wisps of dark hair that straggled over her thin face.

"I don't rightly know where he is," she said wearily. "He took the trap and went off this morning. I thought perhaps he went to

York on some errand."

"I came to see Annie. I've some blackcurrant cordial and some honey, from my aunt."

"Thank you, miss. That was thoughtful of her." Anna Rowe, who knew as well as Lucy did that Trinity Holden took no interest in her son's employees, kept up the polite fiction.

"Emma will be over on Sunday to see how you are," Lucy said.

"That'll be grand. I do miss our Emma."

"But surely — how long is it since you saw her?" Lucy asked carefully.

"About a month, miss. She came over last month to see us all, but she couldn't stay long. I reckon she'd work to do back at Ladymoon."

"Cannot you clean this place up a little? All this dust cannot be good for Annie's chest."

"I try to keep it decent," Anna said, "but I get tired, miss. I get bone-tired and I'm not carrying this babe right. I'm sick all the time and I have a fierce pain in my side.

"I'll have a word with my cousin. I'm on the way to the counting house now. He'll see that Elisha calls a doctor."

"Elisha spends too much money at the ale house to have any spare for doctors," Anna said.

"I'll speak to my cousin about that too." Lucy nodded again, and went out into the fresher air of the garden. Anna Rowe could, she thought irritably, have taken the trouble to lift out the ashes and sweep the floor. The Rowe children were hard workers, but the parents tended to be shiftless.

Perched on the high seat again she turned the vehicle expertly in preparation for the steep descent to the mill, and glimpsed a tall, dark young man loping down the hill.

"Good-morning, Saul. Are you going to the Hollow?" She raised her voice slightly as she waved for he showed signs of hurrying past.

"On my way back now, miss. I've been on the look-out for father but he's sloped off somewhere."

"And I have just paid a call on your mother."

"Charity-visiting, miss? Very proper I'm sure." His mobile face was grave, but the corner of his mouth twitched.

"Ride down with me," she invited. "I'd be glad of a word."

For an instant he hesitated, then swung himself up beside her.

"What kind of a word?" he demanded.

"A friendly one, so you need not glower

48

at me so fiercely. Your mother is not well, Saul."

"She's expecting. It's taken her bad this time."

"And she is neglecting the house. It is quite — dirty, Saul."

"If you don't like it you needn't visit," he said brusquely.

"Cannot the younger ones help?" she enquired. "Mary and Joan are big girls now. And the garden needs weeding and planting. Surely you or your brothers could see to that?"

"The young ones clock on in the weaving sheds at six in the morning and it's past eight when they get in again," Saul said.

"They don't work on Sundays," she interrupted.

"On Sundays they've a three mile walk for the pleasure of hearing Mr Edward preach at them, and in the afternoon they waste their time snaring rabbits and picking berries and catching fish to swell the larder. What leisure is there for dusting and weeding?"

"Cannot one of the girls stay at home?"

"The younger ones get two shillings a week," Saul said. "That's eight shillings, Miss Lucy, and my own wage is seven shillings."

"Your father earns more."

"Aye, two pounds, and half of that is gone on drink before we can wrest anything from him. We need every penny."

"I didn't realise," she said uncomfortably.

"Pretty ladies in yellow gowns are not expected to do any realising," he said.

"Pretty? Do you really think I'm pretty?"

"Aye, very pretty. Like eggshell," he returned.

"I'm really very strong. I've never had a day's illness."

"You look like you'd snap in two if a man put his arm about you."

"I should like to see anyone try," she said flirtatiously.

"Oh, someone will try one day, but it won't be me." He swung himself down to the paving stones as they rattled through the high gates.

"Don't you have a sweetheart, Saul?"

"Not on seven shillings a week," he retorted.

"Everybody thinks too much about money," she said.

"Only when they don't have any. I have to get back to work now."

He had turned away, his shoulders heavy under the darned jacket. His dark hair clustered thickly over his neck. For an instant Lucy saw him clearly as if she had never seen him before and was gripped by a fierce hunger for something she could not understand.

"Saul!" she said loudly.

"Yes, Miss Lucy?" His mouth was twitching again and something at the back of his dark eyes told her that he too was seeing her clearly.

"I like to ride quite far afield sometimes," she said.

"That must be pleasant for you, miss."

"My aunt worries if I ride alone," she stumbled on, "I take one of the grooms with me but they're dull company. If you'd care to borrow one of the horses, one Sunday afternoon?"

"I thought Sundays were for weeding and dusting," he said.

"If you wish to come then we could ride together, if you'd care for it." Her face flamed with angry embarrassment for he stood there stolidly, without helping her out.

"On Sunday then," he said at last. "About two-o-clock."

"We can talk then," she began, but he was striding away across the yard. She stared after him in annoyance, her lip pouting.

The mill was built around three sides of a square. The doors of the weaving sheds were

51

open and she could see the huge looms and hear their ponderous clattering. The counting house was at the far side of the yard, its windows gazing blankly from grimy walls.

"Lucy, my dear! What in the world brings you down here?" Her cousin, Edward, trotted through the gates and dismounted, holding out his hand to assist her down.

"I have a message for Charles. What are you doing here?"

She lifted her skirt clear of the ground as they walked across the yard.

"I have had an invitation from Daniel Lumley to attend a supper party for Sarah." He held the door open for her as they began to mount the stairs.

"So have Aunt Trinity and Charles and me," she said. "I wonder why you had a separate one."

"It was sent to the church. I suppose they expected me to be there. As it happened I'd gone over to check the registers. Are you going?"

"If Charles will accompany me. Aunt Trinity won't stir from home."

"My father's death affected her more than she will admit," Edward said. "Ah, there you are, Charles."

"Where else would I be?" his elder brother enquired, turning from the high desk at which he stood. "Lucy, what brings you here? I saw you from the window a few minutes since, gossipping with Saul Rowe."

"I went to see Anna. She's not well and she's worried on account of Elisha drinking so much."

"You've no business to be running in and out of other folks' houses," Charles frowned. "You could catch something."

"I'm too old to catch croup," Lucy informed him. "I wish you would speak to Elisha. He drinks half his wage away, and in working hours."

"What he does with his money is his own affair," Charles said, "and when he's here he keeps the rest in order. Anyway I sent him over to Halifax, on private business for me."

"Saul wondered where he was."

"Saul ought to have remained on the premises," Charles said. "I'm not obliged to give every millhand an account of the instructions I give to my overseer."

Lucy's heart sank a little. With Charles in a bad humour, her prospects of attending the supper party seemed remote. When she handed over the invitation however his brow cleared, and he said with surprising readiness, "Why we'll certainly go, if you wish it. Does mother favour the idea?"

"For me, but not for herself. Will you really take me? I haven't been anywhere for ages."

"So you begin to crave the fleshpots! Are you invited to this great event, Edward?"

"My invitation came to the church."

"Will you go? It's four years since we saw the lovely Sarah."

"She is not so lovely," Lucy said scornfully. "Her complexion is sallow, and she is far too tall."

"Would you like a glass of milk?" Charles enquired. "Or shall I pour it out into a saucer for you?"

Lucy laughed, but looked slightly ashamed.

Edward poured himself a glass of port from the decanter on the side table and sipped it thoughtfully.

Charles, pushing aside a pile of documents, said, "You are drinking before noon, my dear brother, which means you have something on your mind apart from supper party invitations. What is it?"

"Rumour," Edward said.

"Rumour of what?," Charles enquired.

"Talk has it that new frames are being introduced into the mill."

"Talk runs ahead of action then. It's not past the discussion stage yet, but the new frames are being tried out in Halifax."

"Where Elisha has gone as spy on your behalf?"

"The new frames can be worked by two men instead of six in half the time."

"They'd cost money."

"But we'd recoup the investment within a few months with the saving on wages and the work is three or four times speedier so we'd make more cloth."

"What about the men laid off? You'd pay compensation?"

"We'd come to some arrangement," Charles said easily. "Anyway it'd not be for a year or so. I'm not such a fool as to rush into something like this without due thought. You'll not mention it."

"I've more pressing matters on my mind," Edward said. "The elections are in May and there's talk of Lumley getting on the council. Do we want that?"

"It makes no odds as far as I'm concerned."

"There is talk that he's flirting with Methodism."

"Upon my soul, but I never met a man who took so much heed of — *talk*!" Charles exclaimed. "You ought to pray more and heed less."

"Why don't you stand for the seat yourself?"

"Because politics bore me. Anyway I'd

need to spend half my time in York."

"You do that already," Lucy pointed out. "Aunt Trinity says you spend half your nights in the stews, and it's time you settled down with a decent lass."

"I'm surprised my mother should mention such matters to a young girl," Edward said.

"You'd be astonished at the lewdness of respectable ladies when they're curling their hair in front of the fire," Charles said. "I'll marry when I find a wife who'll let me spend half my time in York."

"You'd stand a better chance of election if you were wed," Edward said. "They like a man who is either respectably married or a respectable widower."

"I told you. I'm not interested in standing."

"Nor much interested in anything else either," Edward said, his tone decidedly nettled. "The cottages are looking very shabby."

"Can I help it if the occupants don't bother to keep them decent?"

"As landlord it's your responsibility to mend roofs and fences," Edward said. "Father took a pride in those dwellings."

"Then it's a pity the tenants don't," Charles said.

"Perhaps they're too tired," Lucy ventured.

"Most of them work a fourteen hour day as it is."

"Hark at the little reformer!" Charles reached out and tweaked one of her curls. "Since when did you begin to take an interest in the working classes?"

"I have eyes," Lucy said.

"And very bright ones too that would be more gainfully employed in needlework or reading improving tales," her cousin said.

"The houses are very damp," Edward said. "The ones at the end of the street are particularly bad. When the level of the river rises there's a tidemark round the outer wall."

"You don't mention that the rents have not been increased for the last ten years," Charles said. "You don't mention that every child gets a pair of boots and an overcoat on the day it starts in the mill, and that a woman gets three full weeks off on half pay when she's confined. And it seems to me they're confined very often. These village woman breed like rabbits. You'd have me spoonfeed them, I daresay. You'd do better to stick to your preaching!"

"I also have sick visiting to do." Edward said stiffly. "The conditions are bad, Charles. Not just in this mill but in others too. The price of food has risen because of the French

57

blockade and wages haven't kept pace. There are families who never see meat from one week's end to the next. Many children have rickets."

"Manufacturers have been hard hit too," Charles said. "Trade has dropped, as you very well know."

"Not so much that you need to count the pennies," Edward retorted.

"You look after your church," Charles said with immense patience, "and I'll look after the mill, and Lucy here — what will you do, Lucy?"

"Go home and bring out my new dress," she said promptly. "Oh, and scold Emma too. She had the afternoon off last Sunday to go and help at home, but Anna hasn't seen her for a month."

"The lass is probably walking out with someone, so let her be," Charles said.

"She wants this Sunday off too."

"Then let her have it, unless you want her for something or other."

"No, I can spare her."

Lucy twisted the strings of her bag round her wrist. "I'll likely be going riding," she said. "With the winter over I think I need more fresh air. Saul has agreed to accompany me, if you have no objections."

"Ride with whom you choose, if it amuses

58

you. Have you done preaching, Edward, because if so I want you to cast your eye over these accounts."

Dismissed, she rose without resentment. Her cousins were together, fair heads bent above the account books. Long legged, wide shouldered, they made a handsome pair. It was a wonder they had escaped marriage for so long, Charles being past his mid-thirties and Edward only four years younger. Another woman in the house would be agreeable, for there were no young girls of her own station within walking distance.

Coming out into the yard she noticed irritably that there were flecks of soot on her yellow cape. She ought to have had better sense than to put on such light coloured garments. After all it was not as if she had gone out with the intention of meeting anyone important. Turley, one of the weavers whose girl, Jessie, worked up at Ladymoon was waiting to speak to her. A lean, anxious looking man, whose wife was said to have the sharpest tongue in Yorkshire, he pulled at his forelock nervously.

"If tha could spare a word, Miss Lucy?"

"What is it, Tom?"

"It's none of my business, but Mr Charles is that busy there's no time to get him alone."

"Get him alone for what?" She accepted his help up to the driving seat.

"Our John, Miss Lucy. Mr Charles said he'd take the lad into York, to see the doctor about his leg. It's a month and more since he promised, miss, but the knee's swelled up so bad I fear the bone's rotting."

"My cousin will have let it slip his mind," Lucy said.

"I'm not getting on at him, miss," Turley said hastily, "but my Martha says she'll be down here to have a word herself if I don't look sharp to it. I'd not want that, miss."

"Is John working?"

"Yes, miss. He brings in two shillings a week, but he's slowed down since he got this gammy leg. Sometimes he cries when we get him up to go to work. Martha won't stand for it much longer."

"You should have talked to Mr Edward," Lucy said.

"As to that, miss, I didn't wish to trouble him, for I don't go to his church."

"You're a Methodist, aren't you?"

"We go to Revival meetings," Turley said. "Mr Charles doesn't object, for he knows I work well, but I'm sore troubled about the lad."

"I'll see what can be done," Lucy promised.

She fumbled in her bag and produced a coin, but the man stepped back reddening.

"I'm not wanting charity," he began, but she interrrupted swiftly.

"It's for holding the pony while I was in the counting house."

"Then I thank thee, miss." He pulled at his forelock again as she clicked her tongue to the docile animal.

Sunday was a fine, bright day. Not until she was dressed in the dark sage habit with its snowy cravat and the little feathered hat did Lucy admit to herself that she had taken particular trouble with her appearance. She was not sure why she had bothered for Saul Rowe was not, by any strength of the imagination, an intimate friend, but he had noticed she was pretty. Thinking of that she began to feel even prettier.

Saul was already mounted and talking to his sister who, in best bonnet and shawl, was preparing to set off for her afternoon out. He broke off as Lucy appeared and came politely to help her into the saddle, his expression betraying neither admiration nor displeasure at her appearance.

"There is seed cake and plum preserve for you to take to your mother," Lucy said briskly to Emma. "My aunt wishes you to be back by seven."

"Thank you kindly, miss. I know my mother will be glad of anything."

Emma spoke in her usual demure manner, dark eyes downcast. For a girl who intended cleaning up a house she was certainly gaily clad, with a bunch of red cherries decorating the brim of her bonnet and gay tartan ribbons on her dress. Lucy wondered if she ought to utter some word of warning, but she had no wish to appear overbearing in Saul's presence and Emma, she supposed, was entitled to have a sweetheart.

"We'll go up on the moors," she told Saul. "As far as Romany Crag and back, will give us a good appetite for supper."

"Wherever you please, miss," he answered her stolidly. She bit her lip, clapped spurs to her mount, and galloped, ahead. Rather to her chagrin Saul caught up with her easily riding the big roan stallion she had ordered to be saddled for him with a casual assurance.

"I didn't know you could ride so well," she called into the wind.

"I like to ride." He turned a flushed face towards her. "It's not often the chance comes my road."

"We must do this again," she began, but he was drawing ahead of her, his back bent over the saddle.

They galloped together in an unspoken

race, the turf scattering clods of earth under their flying hooves, the warm breeze whipping back their hair.

When they drew rein she cried out, "A draw! A draw!"

"Aye, and the poor beasts all lathered up." He dismounted and came to help her.

"We'll rest awhile." She sat down on a grass-covered mound and looked about her at the rolling landscape. Over to the right the dark crag reared up like some prehistoric creature awakening from a green sea.

"It's a lovely view," she said.

"Aye, it's bonny." His eyes travelled slowly from the tip of the white feather to the toe of her green suede boots.

"Will I do?" she enquired, her green eyes teasing.

"You'll do very well, miss." He sat beside her, lifting his face to the sun. The column of his throat was strong and brown, a pulse throbbing under the sunburned skin.

"I wish you would call me Lucy, when we come riding," she said impulsively.

"If you wish." He sounded indifferent.

"We will come riding again, won't we?"

"If you wish."

"You're not very friendly," she complained, tapping her foot impatiently.

"I said I'd ride with you," he said, "but

I didn't know that you wanted friendliness too."

"If you didn't want to be friendly, why did you come?"

"I was curious," he said insolently, "to find out why you decided to take me up."

"Take you up?" She stared at him.

"Like you've taken up charity visiting," he said. "The village is practically drowning in all the soup you've been giving out. And John Turley's to go into the infirmary to have his leg treated. You spoke up about that too."

"Is that wrong?"

"It's very good of you, Miss — ."

"*Lucy!*"

"Lucy, then. Names make no odds. same as soup won't cure rickets and we all know John Turley's due for the burying before summer's out. It makes you feel good and grand to help the poor, I suppose. And it amuses you to take me up, to invite me to ride with you. But it makes no odds. Come morning, I'll be back in the weaving sheds and you'll be up at Ladymoon Manor, counting up your charities."

"I do what I can," she said, her voice trembling. "And you're wrong about me. You know that I came penniless here, that the Holdens took me in. My mother was a poor clergyman's daughter and my father

64

never had two pennies to rub together."

"Then don't jump back into the gutter," Saul said roughly.

"All I wanted was friendship." She plucked bits of grass nervously, her eyes downcast.

"Then you may have it, but I'll not be a toy for an idle afternoon."

"You're insulting!" She rose so quickly that her heel caught in the hem of her skirt.

"I'm your friend." He had jumped up and was steadying her.

For a moment only she swayed towards him. Then he released her and whistled for the horses.

2

Holden Hall stood at the end of a long avenue of trees and was surrounded by parkland. Yew and box had been shaped into fantastic knights and horses, but there were so many of them that the overall effect was sinister rather than gay. The house itself was a huge, unlovely building less than a hundred years old. High walls hid it from the moorland and within it was dark and echoing, its corridors and apartments dominated by suits of armour and cases of stuffed owls collected by a previous owner. Sarah Lumley stood next to her father to receive the twenty or so guests whom he had invited to the supper party. She had been at home for less than a month and was already restless. In London there was a constant round of social gaiety and though the wars with France had resulted in certain shortages there was no lack of dashing military gentlemen to partner one at dances. It was unfortunate that the only proposals of marriage she had received had been from unsuitable candidates. Sarah, even more than her father, set great store by birth and breeding.

Tonight she looked at her best, white shoulders rising from the low cut bodice of a pink gown. Rose diamonds encircled her high-piled black hair and long slim neck.

It was a pity, she thought, glancing at her father that as he grew older he showed his origins more plainly. In London she had contrived to pass herself off as of Spanish descent, but her father's tightly curled white hair and lined mahogany face betrayed the lie.

Daniel Lumley, unlike his daughter, was proud of his past. Born on a plantation, son of its owner and an attractive half-breed, the decline of the Lumley fortunes had led to his being sold and shipped to Liverpool. He had been a young man then, and now he was an old one, but his basic philosophy of life remained unchanged. Through a combination of circumstances he had obtained his freedom and acquired Holden Hall. It was now a thriving estate and Daniel Lumley was a respected citizen with an excellent chance of being elected to the Council. He had married comparatively late in life, choosing a respectable young woman whose pale skin and light hair would mitigate his own swarthiness. She had lost her life in giving birth to the child who was his one weakness. For Sarah nothing could be too good or too expensive. She was one of the most elegant and accomplished young women in the neighbourhood, and the fact that at twenty-four she was still unmarried was, in his opinion, only a tribute to her good sense.

The guests were filing in, a trifle self-conscious for few of them had visited Holden Hall socially. During Sarah's absence in London Daniel had done any necessary entertaining in York. Tonight however spring flowers were piled in elaborate arrangements around the walls and log fires blazed on the wide hearths.

"Miss Lucy, I'm so pleased you were able to come. You remember my daughter, Sarah?"

"Yes, of course. Welcome home, Miss Sarah."

Lucy, red curls clustering over her small head, was in white gauze, its high waist piped with green velvet, its short train embroidered with silver. Daniel shook hands with her cordially, wondering if her cousin had any thought of eventually marrying her. Probably not, for the girl had no dowry at all, and Charles was not likely to be interested in such familiar fruit.

"I was sorry your aunt was not able to

come," he said sincerely.

Trinity had been a lovely girl and her marriage to Matthew Holden had fulfilled her. He had sent his condolences on the latter's death but it was years since he had taken with Trinity herself, though at one time they had been close friends.

"My aunt is becoming something of a recluse," Lucy said.

"A pity, for she deprives old friends of the pleasure of her company. You will be sure to convey my respects to her?"

"As she does to you, sir."

Lucy dipped into a graceful curtsey and passed on into the main salon. There was space here for enthusiastic dancers to form a set, the music being provided by a quartet already tightening up in the minstrels' gallery. Through the double doors at the end of the salon long tables, piled with food were arranged. Lucy, who had a hearty appetite, glanced longingly at the spiced meats and jewel bright jellies.

"Do you care to dance, Mr Charles?"

Sarah had moved away from her father and was smiling at the tall, fair-haired man.

"If my partner is a very beautiful young lady called Sarah Lumley," he bowed.

"Thank you for the compliment, sir. I

wish it were true, but I am cast quite in the shadow by your cousin. How lovely she looks!"

"Lucy looks well enough." He threw her an indifferent glance.

"How ungallant of you, sir. Perhaps it's fortunate for me that I never had a brother or a cousin. I find Miss Lucy most piquant."

"Do you indeed?" He looked at her with amusement. "In that case you must cultivate her friendship. It is not often we have visitors at Ladymoon Manor."

"Are you inviting me to call?"

"Lucy and my aunt would be delighted to welcome you."

"Then I shall stay away," she said, "for you make it clear that you would not welcome me."

"On the contrary I did not mention it lest my feelings caused me to overleap the bounds of propriety."

Sarah blushed prettily, raising her feather fan to her mouth. Her lips were full and red, with a sensual droop to the lower one that fascinated him. He had always thought of Sarah as the rather colourless daughter of a man he secretly envied and despised, but her years in the south had improved her. And she was the future mistress of a house he had always craved.

Sarah, fingertips resting lightly on his arm as they took their places in the set, was aware of his interest. He was, she considered, a personable man, not titled or as wealthy as her own father, but a coming man. Long lashes shielding narrow brown eyes she permitted a gently inviting smile to touch the corners of her lips.

"So you will stand in the local elections, sir?" Edward, who disliked dancing, sipped port and eyed his host speculatively.

"The matter is not settled, though I've been approached. I was flattered to be considered."

"Yes, indeed." Edward's tone subtly conveyed his opinion.

"If I do stand it will be because I hope to do some good by it," Daniel said.

"To better social conditions? I am at one with you there, sir. They can stand improvement."

"Your brother doesn't share your views, I take it. I've heard that he intends to lay off some of his weavers."

"Not yet, if at all. The new looms have not yet been tested properly. Charles will not rush into anything unless it promises a good return, and he will not lay off workers without ensuring them fair compensation."

"I am glad of it, sir, as you must be.

I'm sure that in your calling you see much misery."

"Too much," Edward said sombrely. "I do what I can, but it is not easy."

"And the indiscriminate giving of alms does little to help the overall picture of social unrest. It is there, Mr Edward, seething like oil coming up to the boil in a cauldron."

"You speak as if you feared revolution," Edward said.

"I fear anarchy more. There are some revolutions that men of sense and compassion would welcome."

"You sound as if you were soliciting my vote," Edward said.

"Surely you will vote for your brother."

"Charles does not intend to stand for election. He has no interest in politics, so you have one rival the less."

"I would have welcomed a fight," Daniel said. "My age and experience against a younger man. An interesting combination."

"Not a fair one," Edward said. "Charles has a considerable amount of influence."

"While I am still remembered as the mulatto, born in slavery? Perhaps." Daniel gave the young man a long, level look, then said. "We must not leave the ladies to their own devices for too long. Julia Trowbridge and her mama have been glancing in our direction these five minutes. There will be cards later for those who don't care to dance."

No expense had been spared to make the evening an enjoyable one. Yet Lucy, dancing with one or other of the young men, was conscious of a vague dissatisfaction. Exchanging polite banalities, pointing her toes and arching her head as her partner circled her in the measure, she had a feeling of unreality, as if the walls were about to dissolve and leave them all dancing in the cold wind that swept across the moors.

"May I offer you a glass of champagne, Miss Lucy?" Her host was bending his white head towards her.

"I think I've had too much already," she confessed.

"Perhaps you would prefer some fresh air? I would be happy to lend my escort, if you don't object to the company of an old man."

"Oh, I like old gentlemen," she said with cheerful tactlessness. "I'll just get my wrap."

It was of white velvet, and her curly head emerging from its trig collar was like the calyx of some exotic flower rising from shielding white petals.

"It's a fine night," he observed, as they

stepped out to the terrace.

"The moon is rising." She tilted her head to gaze at its pale orb.

"I take it that the moon attracts you?" He drew her arm through his as they began to pace down the steps into the darker walk beyond.

"I like the sun too," Lucy said, "but I freckle in it and the tip of my nose peels. The moon is gentler."

"And softens reality? You are a dreamer, my dear."

"That is what my cousins say, but everyone should have a dream," she said earnestly.

"And what is yours?"

She hesitated, while for reasons she could not understand there flashed into her mind a picture of Romany Crag with the two horses grazing at its foot.

"Dreams are not always for the telling," she said at last.

"Except to the moon? Miss Lucy, you are wiser than your years."

He looked down at her kindly, hoping that life would not hurt her too much. There was a quick-silver quality about her that could be so easily diminished.

"I am not wise at all," she said with a little gurgle of laughter. "Sometimes I'm as giddy as a goat Aunt Trinity says, but she laughs when she says it. And there are times when I feel so sad that the whole world weighs me down. My mother used to tell me when I was little that it was because I was born with the sun in Pisces, but I think I have the moon in Pisces too."

"That's likely," he said gravely. "Was your mother interested in such things?"

"I believe so. She died when I was five. Your parents — " She stopped, a little embarrassed.

"My father was a gentleman, with no sense save that of honour. After his death the full extent of his debts was discovered. My mother was a very beautiful girl, very gentle. She was — a lady. Does that seem a strange thing to say of a woman born into slavery?"

"No. It sounds a true thing to say," she returned softly.

"You're a sweet child, Miss Lucy." He patted her hand absently as they turned the corner and continued their slow walk. At each side of them towered the strangely shaped hedges of box and yew.

A soft gurgle of laughter disturbed their separate thoughts.

Then Sarah's voice sounded clearly, rippled with amusement.

"Mr Charles, if you persist in saying such

things to me I shall have to return to the house!"

"Where you will dance with other men and cause me some twinges of envy?"

"Only twinges, sir? Most gentlemen would have said agonies."

"I am not like most gentlemen, Miss Sarah. I always speak the literal truth."

Her laughter rang out again, high with a note of excitement as she exclaimed, "And that, sir, is the first lie you have told!"

Daniel Lumley turned and began to walk back towards the house. After a moment or two he said to Lucy. "Is your cousin an agreeable man? Is he kind to you?"

"Very kind, sir. He regards me more as a sister than anything else."

"And Mr Edward?"

"Is very correct," Lucy said. "He's a great hand at praying, you know."

"Is he indeed? You sound as if you don't approve," Daniel said.

"I don't mind it," Lucy said tolerantly, "but words don't reach far, and they don't always mean what folk think they mean. Prayer is more like a feeling inside me, and it doesn't come in church. In church I'm wondering if Cook will remember to put the nutmeg in the pudding, and thinking how nice Edward's new surplice looks, and it's not like praying at all. But when I'm out on the moors, or down by the river, that's like a prayer and there aren't any words at all."

"You're a pagan, Miss Lucy."

They had reached the foot of the steps and he looked down at her in amusement. "That can be an uncomfortable thing to be in this day and age. I hope you are not hurt or disappointed by people who don't understand."

She was not sure exactly what he meant, but his voice was kind, so she smiled up at him and said politely, "Thank you, sir."

Edward took her into supper. Her cousin, she thought, seemed even graver and more thoughtful than usual. He had not danced or paid much attention to the other young ladies, but she noticed him glancing about him with a look on his face that she could only describe as calculating.

It was not until they were rattling home in the closed carriage that was used only on rare occasions that Edward gave some hint of his musings.

Glancing across at his brother who sat opposite, he said, "You appear to have made quite an impression upon Miss Sarah, Charles. I saw you talking to her most of the evening."

"She has improved out of all recognition

since going to London," Charles said.

"Indeed she has. There is a certain brilliance about her that is very noticeable."

"Are you thinking of cutting me out?" Charles enquired.

"Sarah Lumley would not take a second look at a clergyman," Edward said.

"Neither would her father take a second look at a millowner," observed Charles.

"Four years ago I might have agreed with you, but Sarah has not succeeded in netting a title. He may be content to see her fly for lower game."

"She is certainly handsome," Charles said thoughtfully.

In her own corner Lucy sank deeper into her velvet cape and closed her eyes. The motion of the carriage, the low well-modulated voices of the two men, the sighing of the night wind all combined into a rhythm that made her pleasantly sleepy.

Somewhere beyond the fringes of sleep were other noises. Fierce yells and screams broke upon her ears and the sound of rifle shots pittered through the air. She could hear men running and a crashing, rending noise as if axes were being used with great force. She screamed out herself, and was suddenly awake, with Charles shaking her and Edward leaning forward, his face alarmed.

"In God's name, Lucy, what ails you?," Charles demanded.

The carriage was pulling to a halt and Jem's voice came, rough and apprehensive.

"What's amiss, master? Is one of you hurt?"

"Miss Lucy fell asleep and had a nightmare," Charles called, lowering the window and sticking his head out.

"I wasn't asleep," she protested. "There were men running and shooting and noise, everywhere noise."

"Too much champagne," Edward pronounced. "Leave the window open, Charles. Better a draught than the horses bolting!"

They moved on again, wind filling the compartment, ruffling the curls on Lucy's head, banishing sleep. Or had it been sleep? She was no longer certain and the memory of it was fading.

In the weeks that followed life resumed its normal course. Lucy thought, with a touch of wistfulness that it was only in novels that the heroine went to a ball and was swept off her feet by some dashing young man. In reality one enjoyed a good supper, danced several times, thanked the host politely and came home.

"I wish you could have seen my gown," she told Saul when they rode together. "All white and silver with a border of green, and new green slippers too. Aunt Trinity sent to York ages ago for it to be made but I'd no opportunity to wear it until the supper party. Everything was so elegant at Holden Hall. Big log fires and a quartet and smoked salmon brought all the way from Hull. Saul, do stop scowling and listen to me!"

"I'm in an ill humour," he said moodily.

"With me?" She prepared to pout prettily, but he said. "Nay. You'd put me in a good humour if anyone could! It was John Turley I was thinking about."

"John? — oh, the little lame boy. I'd forgotten about him."

"He'll be forgotten by all soon," Saul said. "He died over at the infirmary."

"I didn't know that." Wrenched from the enticing thoughts of new clothes she stared in sympathy. "My cousin arranged for him to go there."

"With the best intentions, but the tumour was far advanced. It was bound to happen."

"I'm sorry about it."

"No sorrier than his parents," Saul said bitterly. "Johnny was bringing in two shillings a week. Mind, with him gone there's a mouth less to feed."

"I'll go and see his mother," she promised.

"With more soup?" He gave her a wry glance.

"Why is it that I can never do anything right in your eyes, Saul Rowe? Was it my fault the boy died?"

"No, and it wasn't your fault he was born into an overcrowded, ill-lit, badly ventilated cottage, with an open cesspit not ten yards from the door; nor that he lacked the meat and milk that would build up strong bones and teeth; nor that he was put into a mill at the age of five, and he had no doctor near him until it was too late to help. It's the fault of the system, Lucy, and until that's altered there'll always be a John Turley in every village; more than one in most."

"How can it be altered?," she asked.

"The masters could make a start," he said. "They could raise wages to match living costs, lower rents, and shorten hours."

"Charles said that if he did that his profits would fall and he'd not be able to pay his millhands," Lucy argued.

"His profits are big enough already," Saul said. "He has a fine house and a string of fine horses, and he keeps his mother and cousin in idleness."

"I suppose you'd have me working at the looms," she said.

"I'd not have you any different from the

81

way you are," Saul said. "I don't grudge you any of your pretty clothes, or your parties. I wish more could have them, that's all. The masters won't see to it, so the men must. The changes are pressing up from below, and won't be held down much longer."

"That's dangerous talk," she said uneasily.

"Talk's cheap," Saul said. "It's action that's needed."

He spoke as if he were impatient not only with the conditions against which he inveigled but with himself.

They had ridden out to Romany Crag and were sitting on the warm grass. The sun, sparkling overhead in a blue sky dotted with fluffy white clouds, sent gleams of gold dancing in Lucy's red curls. She had removed her hat and curled its feather over her fingers as she listened.

Saul, who had been pacing up and down, stopped and looked at her, a rueful smile lighting his sombre face.

"You must find me dull company," he said. "You invite me to come riding and I repay you with a lecture on social inequality."

"Oh, everybody lectures me," Lucy said placidly. "My aunt lectures me on the dangers of wandering about down in the Hollow. Cousin Edward lectures me on the state of my soul, and Cousin Charles lectures me about practically everything else. I pay them no heed, but what you say interests me. It truly interests me and makes me want to help in some way, but there isn't anything I can do."

"Listening helps me," Saul said. "You listen more intently than anyone I ever met, as if your whole mind is concentrated upon what I say."

"But I forgot about John Turley," she said contritely.

"So has everyone else." He came over and leaned to help her to her feet.

Always, when she stood close to him, she was conscious of his height and strength. She could smell the strong male scent of him that excited her in a way she couldn't clearly understand. Usually he moved away, but today he stood still, looking down at her.

"I'd like to see you in that white and silver gown," he said, and his deep voice was softly slurred as if he too felt an inner excitement.

"I'll wear it for you," she said.

"When? Where?"

"Down by the river tonight, after the moon has risen. I'll wear it for you then." Her own voice trembled and her eyes gleamed green, as if she had set before him unimaginable delights.

"Tonight then," he said almost curtly and turned away, to call the grazing horses back to them.

The rest of the day went too slowly. Her ride over, she changed into a high-necked gingham dress and sat obediently in the parlour, listening to Aunt Trinity ramble on about her own childhood.

"That was in America, of course, when it was still a colony. I can recall my grandmother. Catriona Bostock was her name and she was a Cornishwoman, very dark though in those days ladies powdered their hair and wore hooped skirts that were held out at the sides. A very graceful fashion, my love, and I'm sorry that it passed. These narrow skirts only flatter ladies with perfect figures."

She glanced rather sadly at her own plump figure and helped herself to a chocolate by way of consolation.

At supper there were only the two of them. Edward generally spent the weekend over at the church. It had a two-roomed cottage attached to it, and he slept there, working out his parish visits for the next week, making notes on his sermon. Charles was in York and had sent word he'd not be back until Tuesday.

"Though I do suspect he will break his

journey at Holden Hall. Edward tells me that Charles was most attentive to Sarah Lumley on the evening of the supper party."

"He seemed to admire her," Lucy said.

"We must invite her here, perhaps give a little party for you. If Daniel Lumley can do it for his daughter then I can surely do the same for my niece. When your birthday comes we could arrange a celebration."

"I had a birthday in March," Lucy said.

"Did you, dear? I'd quite forgotten." The grey eyes blinked at her vaguely. "Perhaps we can find some other reason for a party then. This year I do intend to bestir myself and chaperone you into society. You are a very pretty girl and ought to have more gaiety in your life."

She would not, Lucy knew, actually do anything at all. She would enjoy making plans for a day or two, and then she would drift back into the misty half-world she had occupied ever since her husband's death.

On most evenings she retired after supper to the great bedchamber she had shared with Matthew, but on this evening she lingered over the meal, talking pleasantly, telling Cook to brew a cup of tea so that she and Lucy could enjoy an hour or two together by the parlour fire.

At last, however, as the clock struck

nine, she yawned and heaved herself out of the comfortable armchair in which she had ensconsced herself, her draped gown floating about her.

"Are you going up now?" she enquired.

"Not yet, It's such a warm night I might step out into the garden for a while," Lucy said.

"Put on your warm cloak then, my dear," Aunt Trinity advised. "You won't go beyond the garden, will you? One can never be sure these days."

"I'll tell Cook to leave the door on the latch," Lucy promised.

"Very well then. Goodnight, my dear." Aunt Trinity kissed her affectionately, scooped up a bunch of sugared grapes, and went out.

Lucy waited until she heard the closing of the door and then hurried up to her own room. The dress of white and silver hung limply on its hanger. She took it down, wriggled out of the gingham dress, and slipped the balldress over her head. It was, she thought, the loveliest gown she had ever had.

Her white velvet cape around her shoulders she went down the stairs again, pausing at the kitchen door to instruct Cook to leave the main door on the latch.

It was, as she had expected, warm in the garden and silvered by the rising moon. She stood for a moment, breathing the fragrance of night scented stock. By day she felt brisk and gay, but at night a langour stole over her as if some unseen presence had brushed her with its wings. She walked slowly across the lawn, her head raised a little to the starhung sky. She felt mysterious and feminine, as if the world had retreated and she moved in a universe that she herself had created.

Beyond the gate the ground sloped sharply down to the river. Further along she glimpsed an occasional light twinkling from one or two of the cottages, but most were in darkness. The millworkers went early to bed. The moon shone so brightly on the river that its surface was like silver. She gazed at it, her lips curving into a smile. There was mystery here, as if the rays of the moon had effected a subtle transformation. Her own white cloak shared in the transformation. She raised her arms and saw them as pale stems, the fingers spread like petals, the palms cupped to catch the silver rays.

A taller figure moved out from the trees.

"It is a bonny gown," Saul said huskily.

"Do you truly like it?" She spun around to face him, her cloak spread wide.

"I like better the one who wears it," he said.

"Even if I drown the village in soup?" she asked.

"You may do as you please," he said. "In that dress you may do exactly as you please."

For an instant she hesitated. Then she moved closer, holding out her hands, raising her small face. She could see him shaking his head back and forth, hear him murmur something deep and inarticulate. Her eyelids drifted down over the brilliant green orbs, and her questing mouth found its fulfilment.

Moon and river spun into nothingness and her feelings were of a primitive pleasure beyond anything she had ever imagined.

"This won't do, Miss Lucy!"

Opening her eyes, moving away from him as he moved away from her, she whispered, "Why?"

"It's not fitting," said Saul. "It's not fitting for you and me. Miss Lucy."

"Don't call me 'Miss'," she said. "You told me once not to jump back into the gutter. Now I say to you that you must not stay in the gutter when something is offered to you."

"Something it would dishonour you to offer," he said sombrely.

"You're wrong! Saul, you're wrong!" She came to him again, her hands outstretched, the cloak slipping from her shoulders to lie on the moon-dappled grass. "You're wrong, Saul. If it would not dishonour you to take, then it does not dishonour me to give. Like this, here where there is only the river and the trees, and we have no names. We have no names here, my dear. Nobody has any name, and words don't mean anything. Words never did, you know."

His arms enfolded her again and the thudding of his heart was louder than the wind. She raised her head for his kiss and saw, out of the corner of her eye, something move at the edge of the river where the rushes grew most thickly.

"What is it?" He too had sensed the movement and turned to gaze in the same direction.

"Someone out there, watching us," she whispered. There was another stirring of the reeds, and a figure stood, clear and graceful, in the moonlight. Long hair streamed over narrow shoulders and through the rents of a ragged skirt flashed thighs of greenish white, glinting with drops of water.

Then, abruptly, the moon retreated behind a cloud and the silver fled from grass and river.

"What was it?" Her teeth chattering, she hung to his arm. "Dear God, but what was it? Was it a ghost?"

"There are no such things," he said, but the arm that held her shook perceptibly. "It was one of the village lasses, I wager."

"Did you recognise her? Where did she go?"

"I never saw her before," he said. "She must have run back towards the Hollow."

"I'm cold," Lucy said abruptly.

"I'll get your cloak." He stepped to where it lay, lifted it and wrapped it about her shoulders. His movements were gently protective, all desire fled.

"Perhaps it was one of the nuns who lived in the convent that used to be here," Lucy persisted.

"Three hundred years back. It's not very likely."

"To come so silently!" She shivered, wishing he would put his arm round her again but he said, his voice flatly practical, "I'd best be getting home now. I'll see you to your door."

"No need. I'll run through the garden."

"Up to the gate then?"

"I said there's no need!" Her voice broke with frustration and disappointment. "I'm quite capable of walking a couple of hundred yards without escort."

"Goodnight then." He was as stolid and unemotional as the black stones of Romany Crag.

She nodded curtly, walked a few steps and turned to where he stood watching her through the darkness.

"We will — go riding again, won't we?" she asked.

"On Sunday afternoon," he returned.

It was sufficient. The moon was emerging again, splashing its silver on the water. It was like a promise, and Lucy was in the mood to clutch at any omen.

At the garden gate she turned to wave but he was staring into the water, his head bent. Nothing moved along the banks; only a small wind shook the rushes. The gate was hard and solid under her hand. She clicked it shut and ran across the lawn, skirting flowerbeds and rose-bushes, pushing open the main door.

"Is that you, Miss Lucy? If you'll lock up now I'll stir the parlour fire and bring you a nice hot posset."

Cook's voice, cheerful and practical, dispelled the last remnant of fantasy.

3

"So Daniel Lumley is now on the Council? Are you not sorry you didn't stand against him?"

Edward raised questioning brows across the table at his brother.

"For the privilege of warming a seat in the Council Chamber? Let other men play at politics. I've my business to attend."

"Do you mean the mill or Sarah Lumley?" Lucy enquired pertly. "You've been paying court to her for months."

"Slowly, safely is my motto," Charles said. "Miss Sarah is not a hedge girl to be tumbled."

"Have you asked her to marry you yet?" Aunt Trinity asked with interest.

"She knows that I admire her," Charles returned.

"And admire her house and fortune even more?" There was a faint snap in Edward's voice.

"That too." Unruffled, Charles broke his bread and chewed a piece.

"But you wouldn't live in such a great barn of a place?" his mother questioned.

"I might. Edward could rent Ladymoon Manor from me and build his church nearer."

"And take a wife." Aunt Trinity's mind was evidently running on marriages this morning, for she went on. "And Lucy will probably be wed too in a few years. I like to have children running about the place."

"Lucy isn't interested in young gentlemen," Charles teased. "She spends her leisure in good works."

"And ought not to be mocked on that account." Edward spoke sternly.

"I shall probably be an old maid," Lucy said. "I will divide my time between Holden Hall and Ladymoon Manor, taking care of all the children that are going to be born, and I shall gain a great reputation for saintliness."

"I shall enjoy seeing you do that," Charles said, amused. "They tell me you've made a start already, forever poking about in the cottages, telling everyone how to manage their affairs."

"Which is where I should be now." She rose, pushing back her chair. "I promised to look in on the Rathbones, Mary has a dreadful cough and I've been dosing her with coltsfoot and honey, but she gets no better."

"All the Rathbones are consumptive. It runs in the family," Charles observed.

"Their cottage is very damp," Lucy said earnestly. "When it rains the water runs down the walls and seeps up through the floor. Jenny Rathbone told me the bread goes mouldy in her larder within a day, and, if they leave their boots on the floor, by morning they're full of water."

"Next year, if I can hold the profits steady, I'll see about repairs," Charles promised.

"I'll tell them that." Lucy kissed her aunt and went out to the waiting pony trap.

It was a damp, heavy September day, with the river swollen and rivulets of water running down the unpaved street. At the Rowe house she pulled up to talk to Anna who leaned against the door, listlessly gazing down towards the mill.

Anna had lost the child she had been expecting and, probably at Saul's insistence, had made some effort to improve herself. Her hair was tied back, her skirt neatly darned. At her feet Annie crouched on a stool, playing with a wooden doll.

"Good-morning." Lucy's greeting was cheerful.

"If it's Saul you want, Miss Lucy, he's down in the weaving sheds," Anna returned.

"I'm on my way to the Rathbones. Mary is not well."

"They're none of them up to much." Anna Rowe's voice was weary. "I was over there half the night myself."

"I'll see what can be done. I have some physic for Mary."

"That stuff you gave her last week made her sick," Anna said.

"Oh. Oh, well, we'll have to try something else." Lucy was a little put out at the older woman's tone. It lacked warmth and her eyes were hostile.

"As you please, miss," Anna said indifferently and resumed her gazing.

Lucy spurred the pony into action and drove down the hill to the Rathbone cottage. Like its neighbours further up the street it was a two roomed dwelling with a loft over the outer room. The front door stood open and beyond she could see a jumble of mattresses and iron railed beds. Jenny Rathbone was at the table, cutting vegetables into narrow strips and adding them to the pot which hung over the smouldering fire.

"Good-morning, Jenny." Lucy hesitated on the threshold but Jenny Rathbone's smile was welcoming.

"Do step inside, Miss Lucy. Excuse the mess, but the bairns are not too well this morning, so I'm behindhand."

"What ails them?" Lucy looked round at the three children who were sprawled on the mattresses.

"A bit of a cold, miss. It's running through the family. Mary took bad first and passed it on."

"She looks feverish." Lucy peered more closely at the child's flushed face and heavy eyes.

"Aye, she was really poorly last night, but Anna Rowe came down to lend a hand. I've not had a chance to get to the spinning."

The spinning wheel stood by the window to catch the light. When Lucy had first come to Ladymoon Manor all the spinning had been done in the cottages and then taken to the weaving sheds, but Charles had an extension built the previous year and the spinning wheels removed there.

"It speeds up production," he had explained, "and cuts down the amount of gossiping that goes on."

Only those women who had tiny children worked now in their own homes. The others sat in the long, light shed whose wooden walls vibrated with the constant whirring.

"I brought some more physic for Mary," Lucy said, putting the bottle down on the table. "Mrs Rowe told me that it made her sick though."

"Better out than in," Jenny said philosophically. "It's the close weather, Miss Lucy. We could do with a touch of frost, or a good storm to clear the air."

"I can send some wine down," Lucy offered.

"That's good of you, miss, and I'll not refuse." Jenny broke off as footsteps clumped up the short path. Elisha Rowe's burly frame darkened the doorway.

"Morning, Miss Lucy." Seeing her, he pulled off his low crowned hat. "I've come over to drag these idlers out of their beds."

"They're sick, Mr Rowe." Jenny spoke deferentially. "Didn't Tom tell you?"

"He said they'd summer colds. It'd be a hard world for millowners if his workers took it into their heads to lie idle every time they sneezed," Elisha observed.

"Mary's been sick for weeks," Jenny pleaded. "That's why I got leave to do my work at home."

"I'm not counting Mary." Elisha gestured towards the two boys. "They look fit enough to come in."

"That's nonsense!" Lucy said warmly. "It's obvious they are feverish. Healthy children don't lie about in such a fashion."

97

"Begging your pardon, Miss, but children will lie about anywhere if they're not stirred to it!"

"They'll be back tomorrow," Jenny said.

"Tomorrow's not good enough. Three of my best weavers are off as it is, and I cannot spare more. If your lads are sick then they'll need a doctor's note before they can claim half pay for the time off. And if they've no note then I've the right to fine them three days' pay for each day's idleness."

"I'll speak to my cousin," Lucy began, but Elisha interrupted, his voice as hostile as his wife's had been.

"If you'll excuse me, Miss Lucy, this is my affair and not to do with the master. Come on now, lads! Up on your feet and I'll give you full pay for today even though it's nearly half over."

The boys heaved themselves reluctantly to the floor, their faces sullen.

"They really don't look fit," Jenny said.

"It's you that doesn't look fit, my lass," the overseer said heartily. "You've enough to do with nursing the little lass without having these great lummocks under your feet. I'll keep an eye on them and send them back an hour early if you're fretted. Be off with you, lads!"

They trailed through the door, dragging

98

their feet. Elisha gave a jerky bow and followed.

Lucy, nodding brusquely to Jenny, picked up her skirts and caught the overseer up.

"Those children are not fit to go to work," she began furiously.

"Then their mother should have called a doctor," he said.

"That's ridiculous! How can she afford to send for a doctor for the sake of a fever? She knows well enough what ails them and how soon they'll be over it."

"If they cannot work I'll send them home again," Elisha returned.

"I'll speak to my cousin."

"Mr Charles leaves such matters to me. You may recall, miss, that I'm paid to oversee, not you."

"I'll speak to Saul," she interposed.

"Saul's not at the mill," Elisha said, with ill-concealed satisfaction. "He's ridden over to Clutterhouses to see Bentham, the carter. We've a load of wool due since last week. But complaining in that quarter will get you no joy. Saul's not overseer yet, nor likely to be, for all the fine notions you puff him up with."

"What exactly is that supposed to mean?" She stopped dead, staring at him.

"Our Saul's a man grown and a good

weaver," Elisha said. "Got a bit of education too, for I saw to it that he learned to read and write, but I never put ideas above his station into his head. Now it's, 'I've no time to help out in the garden on account of I have to go riding with Miss Bostock.' 'Tis a shame you cannot leave him be."

"You're impertinent," she said coldly. "I shall certainly speak to my cousin."

"You do that, Miss Lucy, and I'm likely to complain that your meddling distracts our Saul from his work," he retorted.

Further down the road one of the Rathbone children had stopped and was bent over coughing. The smaller boy was trudging on towards the mill gates. Lucy looked from them to the burly overseer and spoke loudly and furiously.

"I hope you get sick, Elisha Rowe. I hope that you get so sick you can't even lift up your head, and you can't get to your work. I hope you get sick and die, Elisha Rowe!"

She scrambled back into the trap without waiting for his reply and drove away, her face as red as her hair.

So Saul's parents thought she was a meddler who encouraged him to get above himself! Elisha Rowe drank half his wages away and Anna Rowe was a slattern. Yet they took it upon themselves to criticize her, to call her a meddler!

Her quick temper was cooling before she realised she had driven past the mill and was on the low, grassy track that led to Clutterhouses. She had not consciously intended to come this way, but now that she was here she might as well continue in the hope of seeing Saul. She drove on more slowly, letting the horse pick its own way along the track.

The cluster of stone houses came into view as she crested the rise, and she drew rein, her keen young eyes scanning the vale. In the square of turf that served as village green she could see Bentham's high wagon piled with bales, and hitched next to it one of the brown cobs used at the mill when anyone was sent on an errand beyond walking distance. The two men must be in one of the cottages, or perhaps in the alehouse at the corner.

Even as she watched two figures emerged from that very building and stood in close, converse. She could see Saul's black head inclined towards the carter's greying one.

A sudden shyness afflicted her. Since the night when she had worn the white and silver dress her relationship with Saul had continued with Saul apparently unchanged in an easy friendship, but she was aware of the depths that lay beneath it. To ride

101

with him on Sunday afternoons was one thing. To drive out in search of him with no valid reason for seeing him was another matter.

She turned the trap around and urged the pony onto the open moor. On all sides the grass rose and fell in waves of grey green merging into lavender and blue where it met the horizon.

Her bad humour was evaporating. The peaceful landscape soothed her troubled spirits. In the distance something moved towards her. She checked the pony and sat, watching the figure come into focus as the distance between them diminished.

The girl was about her own age, a scarf tied over her long hair, her legs and arms sticklike as they emerged from a ragged dress. As she reached the side of the trap she ducked her head shyly, glancing up from beneath dark lashes.

"Are you gathering berries?" Lucy enquired.

"Aye, and roots too." The girl held up a flat basket. "Later I'll snare a rabbit if luck holds out."

"You're not from these parts," Lucy said.

"Nay, from further south." The girl jerked a grubby finger over her shoulder.

"You were down by the river some weeks past, weren't you?" Lucy said.

102

"I wasn't doing no harm," the girl said. "I needed somewhere to sleep."

"Have you no home? What's your name?"

"Esther. Esther Evans, mistress."

"Evans? Are you Welsh?"

"I don't think so," the girl said doubtfully. "We lived there for a time."

"We?"

"The rest of us, moving northward after the winter had gone. The others fell sick or found work."

"And you came on alone?"

"Reckoned I'd make out better by myself," Esther said.

"Are you gypsy?"

"Nay mistress, travelling folk isn't Rom," Esther said. "We don't hang together same as they do. We go with the seasons."

"I see." Lucy, who didn't see at all, frowned at the girl thoughtfully. There was no doubt she was thin and ragged, but she looked healthy enough.

"Have you looked for work," she asked. "The mill — "

"I've never worked in a mill," Esther interrupted. "I'd not like to be shut up in one place."

"Can you clean or sew, wash dishes?"

"Reckon I could." Esther spoke slowly, her eyes still downcast.

"Do you know the big house that stands above the river?"

"I've seen it, mistress."

"If you come there this evening I'll see if there's work for you. If you don't find employment of some kind you're likely to be taken up as a vagabond," Lucy said severely.

"I might come," Esther said at last. "Then again I might not come. But I thank you, mistress."

She ducked her head and darted away again, bending to the low bushes that were spread over the grass.

"Who in the world is that?" Saul, riding up the slope to join Lucy, stared after the figure.

"Her name's Esther. She's one of the travelling folk, she says."

"A tinker," Saul said with faint contempt, "They move from place to place, thieving mostly."

"She said she didn't want to be shut up in a mill," said Lucy. "If she comes up to Ladymoon I'll see if Aunt Trinity will give her employment. Jessie is getting too big to skivvy any longer."

"She looks — " Saul hesitated and then shrugged. "I've probably seen her around the place."

"I suppose so." She flushed a little and clicked her tongue to the horse, but he leaned to curb the rein.

"It's near noon. Why don't you step down and have a bite with me?"

"Up here? I didn't bring anything for a picnic," she said.

"I can ride down to the alehouse and bring something up from there, if you'd choose."

"Yes, yes, I'd like that. There's a dip in the ground over there."

"I'll be back," he said, and cantered away.

The travelling girl was no more than a speck in the distance. Lucy wondered if Saul had remembered the occasion when they had seen the girl and had not mentioned it for fear of embarrassing her.

The hollow was carpeted with tiny harebells, hanging blue heads from shielding green leaves. Lucy laid the blanket over the grass and arranged herself on it, draping her shawl prettily over her shoulders. A moment later she felt ashamed of the impulse and pulled the shawl awry, tugging off the poke bonnet that hid her whiteness from any gleam of sunshine.

"I got ale, fresh bread, cheese, and plums. Will that do?"

Saul dismounted and began to unpack the saddle bag.

"It looks delicious," Lucy said sincerely. "I didn't know I was hungry until now."

"It's more than a lot'll be getting," Saul said.

"I know, but that won't stop me from enjoying it. Is that wrong of me?" She sank her teeth into the tasty crust and nibbled at the cheese.

"I reckon not. What brought you to Clutterhouses?"

"Brought me? Oh, I was in the village earlier. Your father — I met him and he said you'd ridden over here."

"To see Bentham." He nodded.

"So I thought I'd drive over here." Staring at his downbent head she said irritably. "I don't have to ask your leave to drive out on the moors, do I?"

"I'm glad you came," he said. "I'd have been back in the sheds by now if we hadn't met up."

"Why do you work at the looms still?" she asked curiously. "You could go into the counting house. I've heard Charles say that Ben Yarrow is getting too old to be efficient. You could pick up the book-keeping in no time."

"I like the looms better," he said stubbornly. "And I'm not above taking advantage of the fact that as son of the overseer I can come

106

and go more or less as I please. Anyroad, I'd not relish poring over figures all day with Mr Charles breathing down my neck."

"He spends most of his time at Holden Hall these days," Lucy said with a gurgle of laughter.

"With Miss Lumley? There's talk he plans to wed her, if her father agrees."

"I think Daniel Lumley will do whatever his daughter wants."

"She's spoiled then?"

"I think so, but it's not really fair to say. I don't like her very much," Lucy said honestly.

"And you'd not want to live at Holden Hall." He made it a statement instead of a question.

"I'd hate it! I don't ever want to leave Ladymoon Manor," she said decisively.

"I remember when you first came into Yorkshire," Saul said. "You had on a yellow dress and you carried a little trunk. You held onto that trunk as if it were a sword and you were all ready to do battle, but you spoke soft and your lip was quivering as if you didn't know when to smile."

"Fancy you remembering all that," she marvelled.

"Ah, well, it's natural, isn't it?" He bit into a plum.

"Is it? Why?"

"I reckon you know why," Saul said.

"It would be pleasant to be told," Lucy muttered.

"When the time's ripe." He arched the stone away and rose. "I might think about that counting house job," he said after a moment. "At near twenty-two a man has the right to better himself. Have you done eating, or do you intend starting in on the blanket too?"

"I've done." She scrambled to her feet, tying on her bonnet.

"If I go into the counting house, and I've made no promises, mind, but if I did," Saul said, "would you put on that white and silver gown again? In a year, say, if I called up at Ladymoon — "

"I'll not wear it again until you come to call," she said breathlessly.

"Aye, well that's settled then. I'll ride back to the Hollow alongside you. My father'll be roaring like a bull if I'm away much longer."

"Did you know some of the men are off sick? The Rathbone children ought to be at home too, but your father made them go to work."

"One or two were complaining of headache and stomachache." He helped her back into

108

the driving seat and handed up the folded blanket.

"Sick folk ought to stay at home," Lucy persisted.

"To be docked three days' pay unless they've a doctor's note? It's cheaper to go to work," Saul said wryly.

"I suppose so." Looking at him she said. "Life is getting most complicated."

"Life always was," he returned.

As they neared the Hollow a man whom she knew only slightly, as a weaver whose wife had died some months previously, loped out of the open gate towards them.

"Saul! Saul Rowe, you're to run up to the counting house. Your dad's took bad!," he called as he came.

"What's wrong with him?" Saul trotted more urgently.

"A kind of fit. You'd best hurry. Mr Charles sent for the physician," the man called.

"Is there anything I can do?" Lucy addressed the remark to the weaver for Saul had spurred ahead.

"His wife's been sent for, Miss Lucy. And Mr Edward's there with him now," the man said, snatching off his hat.

"I see, You'd better get back then."

"I've leave to go home for an hour. My

sister's not well, and I promised to look in on her."

"What's wrong with your sister?" Lucy asked sharply.

"A touch of fever, miss, but her head ached and she felt sick, so she stayed home. Excuse me, miss." He touched his forelock and loped off.

Lucy bit her lip and stared uncertainly through the gates across the dusty yard. There was no movement at the high window of the counting house and she was shy of intruding.

Then the door opened and Anna Rowe, supported by Edward, came out. Saul's mother was weeping, her face blotched and twisted.

"Lucy!" Edward, seeing her, raised his hand "I'm taking Mrs Rowe home, but you must send Emma down to help. Annie is also sick, I fear."

"What about Elisha?" Lucy asked, but her cousin shook his head with a warning glance.

"He's gone," Anna said in a flat, unemotional tone that constrasted with her ravaged expression. "Died with his face all twisted and his breathing bad. Fifty years old and never had a day's sickness."

"I'll go for Emma." Lucy jerked the reins

110

and set the pony at the steep incline. There was bustle in the street, with several women gathered in a knot of shawls and mob-caps at the corner. One of them intercepted Lucy, laying her hand on the side of the trap, her face and voice full of excited foreboding.

"Have you any news, Miss Lucy? They were saying Elisha Rowe is really poorly."

"He's dead," Lucy said briefly.

"Dead! And him alive only a few hours since! Why, he didn't have the fever, did he?"

"I believe it was a stroke. The doctor will know better when he gets here."

"But you knew before that, didn't you?" Jenny Rathbone had emerged from the group and now raised her voice.

"You stood on this very spot only this morning and called out that you wished him dead. You stood up for my bairns when Elisha nagged them off to the sheds. And Elisha died."

"I have to fetch Emma," Lucy said swiftly.

The women moved aside to allow her to drive past but she could hear the continuing talk as she went up the hill.

"But Emma must go home at once!" Aunt Trinity exclaimed as Lucy finished her tale. "Poor Elisha! She will have to help her mother for a while now."

Emma seemed in no hurry to be gone however. Clad in a bonnet and shawl she stood in the kitchen, a mutinous expression on her face.

"I don't see how I can be spared, miss," she said as Lucy came in. "There's all the apple picking to be done."

"You don't have to pick apples. The girls can see to them."

"Then who's to help Cook?," Emma demanded.

"Emma, your father has died. Your mother will certainly need your help for a few days," Lucy said patiently. "We won't take anything out of your wages while you're away, and you may drive the trap. It's hitched ready, so be off with you."

"Yes, Miss Lucy." Emma bobbed a resigned curtsey and went out into the yard.

"She's not much grief for her father," Cook observed. "Mind, you cannot blame the lass. Elisha's been in drink half the time I've known him. But there! I shouldn't speak ill of the dead. It's hard on Anna — not that he was much of a husband, but his pay was good."

"Perhaps it will be possible to raise Emma's wages so that she can help her mother," Lucy suggested.

112

"If you ask me, anything extra will go on Miss Emma's back," Cook sniffed. "Forever tying her hair in ribbons and flaunting herself before the glass just so that Mr Ch — "

"Just so that Mr Ch — what?"

"Nothing, Miss Lucy." Cook turned a deeper shade of red and began to knead dough with unnecessary vigour.

"Are you saying that she and my cousin Charles are — ?"

"I'm saying nothing that's not my business, Miss Lucy. If the master cares to lead the silly lass on, and she's fool enough to listen, it's not for me to say anything. My lips," said Cook, "are sealed."

Lucy stared at her, her mind tumbling over as new and unsuspected ideas forced their way into her view of life. Emma's frequent afternoons out, her air of sly boldness, had not impressed her as anything more than the airs and graces of a girl trying to ape her betters. There was a coarseness in Emma from which Lucy shrank, but it seemed that gentlemen were different. Charles was past his mid-thirties already and it was not likely that he had lived his entire life in chastity. She had always known that her cousin went into York for his pleasures, but she had never guessed that he might be interested in Emma, or that Emma had encouraged him.

"You had better get on with your work, Cook," she said at last. "Can you make some extra pies too? I shall send them down to Mrs Rowe's, and one to the Rathbones. Mary is sick and two of the lads have a touch of low fever."

"It's been going around for a day or two," Cook said. "There ought to be a storm to clear the air."

"Oh, I almost forgot!" Lucy turned back as she prepared to leave the kitchen. "I've found a skivvy for you. Her name is Esther something or other, and she may come by later. She's a travelling girl."

"A gypsy? I'll not have a gypsy in my kitchen," Cook began.

"No, no, she isn't gypsy, but she has no family and she needs help. She might become a very good worker."

"If you say so, miss," Cook said reluctantly.

"I do say." Lucy went briskly back to the parlour where Aunt Trinity was settling herself for a pleasant gossip about the uncertainties of life.

"Not that I ever liked Elisha Rowe very much, my dear. I told Matthew that he drank too much, but Matthew said he was a good overseer. I didn't press the point for I made it a habit never to interfere down at the mill. Saul is a much more pleasant man, though

I've not spoken to him above once or twice. But his manner was more respectful to me than Elisha's has ever been."

"What was that about Emma?"

They both jumped slightly as Charles came in. He looked tired and drawn.

"Only that Emma has gone down to spend a few days with her mother," Lucy said quickly.

"Yes, I met Emma on her way down. Pour me a drink, Lucy."

"Is something wrong, dear?" his mother enquired. "Apart from Elisha Rowe's suddenly dying, I mean? I suppose it was a stroke? He did drink rather a lot, and I recall telling Matthew — "

"Doctor Fergus certified it as stroke." Charles took the glass and sprawled on the sofa, long booted legs stretched out before him. "While he was in the Hollow I heard him check over some of the millhands. They've been complaining of sickness during the past few days."

"The Rathbone children were not well," Lucy said, "and one of the weavers told me his sister had a headache and sickness."

"The doctor suspects that it may be typhus," Charles said.

"Typhus!" Aunt Trinity sat bolt upright, her beautiful eyes wide with alarm.

"He's not certain, but it looks very much as if it could be. He'll drive back in a few days to see if there are any further cases. Whatever happens we stand to lose. I've twenty of my hands unfit to work already, and a big order just come in from Halifax. Those remaining will have to work round the clock if we are to fulfil our obligations."

"And it wasn't typhus with Elisha?"

"No, mother. A stroke is quite different, but it couldn't have happened at a more inconvenient time. Elisha had his faults but he was a damned good overseer. I've put Saul in charge for the moment. He's young but he has a good head on his shoulders."

"We must help," Lucy said, but Charles interrupted her.

"You're to stay away from the Hollow until the fever is passed, Lucy," he said. "You can send down what comforts are needed, but you must stay away from the cottages."

She opened her mouth to protest, but Cook's voice came from the hall.

"Evans? You don't look Welsh to me! And why cannot you knock on the back door like a good Christian instead of sneaking past the window?"

"Now what is it?" Charles began, looking annoyed.

116

"I engaged a skivvy," Lucy said, rising hastily. "She's a very poor girl, Aunt Trinity, and she's no family or friends. Cook said she wanted a skivvy, and with Emma away we'll need extra help."

"You ought not to engage servants without consulting me," Aunt Trinity said weakly.

"Darling aunt, I would have asked your leave, but with the bad news about Elisha and the sickness, it slipped my mind," Lucy said, planting a kiss on her aunt's smooth cheek. "Do let her stay on a month's trial! I'll be responsible for her, I promise."

"I suppose we can afford another girl?" Trinity glanced anxiously at her son.

"Provided she keeps to the back quarters. I don't want to go falling over strange women all over the house," Charles said irritably.

"I'll see to it myself," Lucy said.

"And not go down to the Hollow until we find how serious the infection is?"

"I promise that too." She blew him a kiss and went out.

Alone, Charles and his mother stared at each other. Then Trinity said, her voice lowered, "So you met Emma?"

"On her way home in the trap."

"Better if she remains away for a little time," Trinity said gently. "With her father dead, and you so friendly with Sarah Lumley, we don't want any — unpleasantness, do we?"

He looked at her sharply, but she was placidly chewing a sugar cake.

4

"So you wish to see me on an important matter?" Daniel Lumley gave Charles a keenly interested look.

"On a private matter, sir." The younger man took the chair offered to him.

"I'll hazard a guess that it concerns my daughter," Daniel said.

"It does." Charles leaned forward, his hands on his knees, and said, "I wish to make her my wife."

"That's plainly spoken like an honest man, at least. What does Sarah have to say?"

"We took the liberty of discussing it," Charles said, "and she is inclined to accept."

"Only inclined? That sounds a mite lukewarm."

"She will not commit herself fully without your permission, sir."

"Very right and proper. Sarah is a dutiful child."

"Then what is your answer, sir?"

"You go too fast." Daniel puffed thoughtfully at his pipe. "You are not a young boy, my friend, but a mature man who has avoided matrimony until now."

"Which is why I am anxious to settle down."

"With my daughter? What makes her so attractive to you?"

"Sarah is an attractive woman," Charles said. "Handsome, cultured and well-educated. Our tastes are similar."

"She will also be mistress of Holden Hall one day."

"I have taken that into consideration, sir, and I'll not deny that it influenced me. Two generations back this estate belonged to my family. My father disliked the place but I have always envied you your possession of it."

"That is frank talk!" Daniel exclaimed.

"It's the truth," Charles said, "and I'll not insult you or Sarah with less. But Holden Hall is only part of my reason. If I had not a genuine affection for Sarah I would not offer for her hand even if she stood to inherit twice over."

"And what have you to offer, apart from a genuine affection?" Daniel enquired.

"As you know, sir, my father left Ladymoon Manor to me, on condition that I gave my mother and my cousin, Lucy, a home there for as long as they wanted one. I also inherited the mill and the cottages down at the Hollow. Of the annual profits from the mill when overheads have been met I take eighty per cent. Edward and my mother have ten per cent each."

"And if you died without issue?"

"Then Edward receives my share in addition to his own, and if he dies without issue then it goes to Lucy. My mother's share will go to Lucy anyway when my mother dies."

Daniel tapped his pipe on the chimney piece and watched the glowing ash flutter down to the hearth.

"What was your net profit last year?" he asked abruptly.

"Eight thousand pounds. My brother and mother received one thousand six hundred pounds and I put four hundred aside for my cousin. My father made no financial provision for Lucy, but I would like her to have a little of her own in the event of her marrying."

"That is generous of you," Daniel approved.

"The manor itself is not a large house, but it is very comfortable," Charles pursued. "If you give your consent, sir, it was our intention to spend part of our time at Ladymoon and part of it here."

"You have already discussed it thoroughly," Daniel observed. "You are, I confess, not the man I would have chosen for my daughter.

When she went to London I hoped — but hopes are often foolish, and it appears that none of the gentlemen there took her fancy."

"The Holdens are a well-respected family," Charles said stiffly. "My father used his own share of my grandfather's inheritance to build the mill and attract labour to it. My mother — "

"Trinity Bostock was a very charming young girl," Daniel interrupted. "I have always had a deep respect for her."

"Then what is your answer, sir? Are you willing to give your consent?"

"There is a further matter." Daniel hesitated, then went on. "We are speaking man-to-man, so I will not mince my words. You are unwed, but not I think, inexperienced. I don't blame you. Indeed it would disturb me if it were otherwise. But Sarah is innocent, and she deserves loyalty. I hope you have no entanglements which might cause your own loyalties to waver."

"I have none at all, sir."

"Then I see no reason why an unofficial engagement should not be agreed."

"Unofficial?" Charles looked disappointed.

"With typhus raging through the village this is not the time for any public celebration," Daniel reproved. "In the New Year, if you are both still of the same mind, then we will make an announcement. You are, of course, free to inform your immediate family."

"And me too, I hope." Sarah came in, impatience in her face, her lips smiling.

"If you are sure of your feelings — " Daniel began.

"Quite sure, father. Having had my London season I am now ready to settle down as the wife of a respected wool manufacturer. May I wear a ring, or must we wait until New Year for that too?"

"I'll have one made for you in York," Charles said.

"A diamond then." Her narrow eyes shone. "One large stone set in gold."

"As my lady pleases." Charles, who had risen at her entrance, kissed her hand.

"Will you stay for supper?" she asked.

"I cannot," he said regretfully. "I gave my word I'd sup at home tonight. My mother knows that I'm here, and she suspects the object of my visit is to propose, so I cannot, in conscience, keep her in suspense."

"Then I'll say goodnight." Sarah linked her arm through his as he bowed to Daniel and began to walk towards the door.

On the terrace he put his arms round her, seeking her mouth, but she turned her head slightly, presenting a cool, sallow cheek.

"You won't forget?" she questioned softly.

"A single diamond set in gold?"

"The finest I can procure," he said gravely.

Her slight recoil did not offend him. After marriage, if her sensual lower lip was a true indication, Sarah would prove a passionate, willing partner. But she would allow him no liberties beforehand.

Mounting his horse, he rode down the main avenue between the strangely shaped trees and bushes, and looked back once to see her poised on the terrace, her hand raised in a graceful salute.

The evenings were drawing in. Already his shadow was long on the grass and the clouds hung low in a leaden sky. He glanced at the reddish horizon and frowned. It was unseasonably warm, and the long awaited storm had not yet materialised. When it did the fever might abate. Half of his best weavers were sick and there had already been a dozen deaths, eight of them children. Profits would certainly fall this year, and he still had orders to meet.

He wondered if it might not have been wiser to have acquired one or two of the new frames. Elisha had been impressed by their demonstration in Halifax, but had advised him to wait a while before committing himself to a purchase. They were expensive to buy and install, and ample compensation would have to be paid out to every man laid off. It was better to wait and see how matters went.

A shawled figure was waiting at the milestone as he rode towards Ladymoon. In the dusk he recognised Emma Rowe and reined in his horse, frowning slightly as she came forward and laid her hand on his stirrup.

"You should be at home, caring for your mother," he said sharply.

"Ladymoon's my home, Mr Charles. Why, I was only nine when I was taken in as a maid," she said, reproach in her face.

It was a broad, rosy face and she had hair and eyes almost as dark as Sarah's; but Sarah's hair was piled high above her thin neck and her eyes were secret. Emma's hair hung thick and greasy over the shoulders of her woollen dress and her eyes held an open invitation and no mystery at all.

"There is need for you at home now," he said more gently.

"To skivvy for my mother who sits nursing Annie and weeping what a saint father was? When he was alive they went at it hammer and tongs about him sneaking off to the alehouse, but now he's gone he was the best man that ever drew breath! I want to come back."

"And carry the infection to my mother and cousin? I cannot permit that."

"Doesn't matter about me then," Emma said resentfully. "A lass like me can catch the fever and die, and you'd not pay it any mind! There was a time when you felt different, Mr Charles. Don't make out it wasn't so, for you and I know better."

"I'm going to be married," Charles said abruptly.

"To Sarah Lumley? She's got black blood, sir!"

"Her grandmother had, but what our parents were doesn't signify."

"Oh, doesn't it though!" Emma flushed scarlet. "If my father had owned Holden Hall and my mother had sat in the parlour drinking coffee, you'd have been glad to walk out with me then! You'd have ridden to take supper with me, then you'd have whispered pretty nothings in my ears. No quick wrestles at the back of the haystack then!"

"Young men flirt," Charles began.

"Flirt! That's a tongue in your cheek word!" she exclaimed. "'Twas more than that and you know it!"

"Whatever it was it's finished," he interrupted. "You ought not to have taken it seriously, Emma."

"Well, I did!" She stood back a little,

hands on her hips, and glared at him. "So what are you going to do about it?"

"Do? Nothing. It's over and done with and almost forgotten."

"Not by me? You can't pick me up and drop me when it suits you," Emma cried.

"That's just what I have done." He gathered up the reins and prepared to move on.

"You could still — visit me." Emma pleaded. "I'd not tell or make a fuss. You could still — "

"I'm going to marry Miss Lumley," Charles repeated.

"I'll tell," she began, but he turned upon her, impatience kindling to anger.

"Tell? Tell what? And who'd believe you? I never gave you any presents or wrote you any letters."

"I never asked for presents, and you know I can't read very well."

"Then it would be your word against mine," he pointed out. "Now be a sensible girl and go back to your mother. Your wages are still being paid."

"They're not enough. With father gone we can scarce manage."

"Then I'll raise them. Look, we'll make a bargain. I will pay you ten shillings a week for as long as you stay with your mother.

That's a generous offer, for I'm not obliged to pay you a penny."

She opened her mouth, but he said roughly. "Take it or leave it. 'Tis all you'll get."

"I'll take it then." She stood with drooping head, eyes glinting beneath lowered lashes.

"That's sensible, lass! Be off home now." He spurred towards the stables.

A pity that he had given his word that he was free of entanglements. Emma was a ripe armful, and their meetings had held the spice of secrecy. But a gentleman's word was his bond and he'd given that word to Daniel Lumley.

His mother and cousin were already at supper when he went in, but it was obvious they were more interested in his news than in the food set before them.

"Is it all settled?" Trinity wanted to know.

"Is all what settled?" He mounted the dais and pulled out his chair.

"You know perfectly well what I mean! Did Daniel give his consent?"

"We are to announce our engagement in the New Year."

"My dear boy, I am so very pleased for you!" Trinity beamed with relief. "I know how much you wanted the match. But why wait until the New Year?"

"The fever will have abated by then

and people will be more in the mood for celebration."

"That's true." She nodded, her face serious for a moment, but her smile broke out an instant later as she exclaimed, "And will you be married from here? We could arrange a very pleasing reception."

"I shall leave those matters to Sarah."

"Who will deal with them very well I'm sure. Do you think she will inform us what colour she is wearing? I'd not wish to clash. And will you live here or at Holden Hall? Your father and I never liked the place, you know, but Daniel will miss his daughter's company."

"We thought to divide our time between the two. I shall still have to run the mill, but as time goes on I shall delegate more of its management to Saul Rowe. He has stepped into Elisha's shoes so neatly that I am only sorry I didn't advance the lad a little before."

"Have you seen Saul?" Lucy had kept her promise not to go down to the Hollow, but could not resist asking.

"I met Emma on the way home. She seems to have her hands full with chores. I was thinking it might be a good idea if we left her there for a time, if you can manage without her?"

"The new girl seems to be shaping well," Trinity said, glancing towards the lower table where the servants sat. "Cook tells me she is obedient and quick to learn. Emma was apt to get above herself, you know."

"I wondered if Saul was well," Lucy said.

"Right as rain," Charles said cheerfully. "With his sister home I fancy the house will be cleaned more often and meals cooked on time."

"Such a pleasant young man," Trinity said. "You will quite miss your rides out on the moor with him, Lucy. Charles, do you think Sarah will invite Lucy to be her bridesmaid? I hope she will, for she has no sisters of her own. And Edward will be your groomsman, I suppose. I wish he would hurry home for he'll be vastly pleased by the news."

"Edward is in danger," Lucy said, so loudly that everybody stopped eating and stared at her.

"In danger? My dear girl, what in the world are you talking about?" Trinity exclaimed.

"All about him is danger," Lucy said in a gasping little voice. The freckles stood out in her colourless face and her green eyes were dilated.

"What kind of danger?" Charles asked.

"All round him like a creeping black cloud," Lucy said.

"Where is Edward," Trinity demanded.

"Down at the counting house. He stayed late to check the accounts. What is all this nonsense, Lucy?"

Lucy's colour was gradually returning but she shuddered violently.

"I saw death waiting for him," she said in a low, strained voice. "Will you please excuse me? I don't feel like any more supper."

Trinity, staring after her niece's retreating figure, said uneasily, "Ought you not to ride down to the Hollow, to make certain Edward is alright?"

"I'll do no such thing," Charles said firmly.

"She spoke so strangely, as if she were looking at something behind her eyes," Trinity said. "You don't think it likely she saw something?"

"More likely that her nose has been put out of joint and she's trying to draw attention to herself," he grinned. "She doesn't like Sarah very much, you know, and she must be a trifle jealous of her coming here as my wife."

"Lucy isn't like that," his mother protested. "She's a very sweet, biddable girl."

131

"Who's been treated as the daughter of the house since she was ten," he retorted. "Now listen, Lucy did this sort of thing once before. On the way back from the supper party at Holden Hall she suddenly screamed out that she could hear men tramping along and smashing up things with axes. She'd had a little too much champagne, I grant you, but Sarah had been very much the centre of attention all evening. Lucy's a sweet lass and I'm very fond of her, but she wasn't born with red hair and green eyes for nothing!"

"You really think so?" Trinity asked doubtfully.

"I'm certain of it. Now, tell me what colour you had thought of wearing. A soft blue would suit you very well and blend with almost any other shade."

Having successfully diverted her thoughts, he settled himself to his meal, with the intention of scolding Lucy when she came downstairs again. But dusk turned to darkness and she did not appear.

In the darkness Emma wiped her eyes on the corner of her shawl and went slowly down the steep rise towards the mill. She had been crying for a long time and her head was aching but when she thought of having to go on living with her mother she wanted to start crying all over again.

Her feelings for Charles ran much deeper than she herself realised. Ever since she had been engaged as a maid at Ladymoon Manor, instead of being put into the mill like most of the other village girls, she had hero-worshipped the tall, fair-haired young man even though he seldom noticed her except to yell for his boots. She had allowed the fumbling caresses of the local lads, closing her eyes so that she could imagine it was Charles Holden who touched her.

Then a year before he had stopped yelling at her and begun watching her as she went about her duties. And from all that had come those hours of unimaginable delight which had ended with his betrothal to Sarah Lumley.

It was not, she thought angrily, as if she had ever asked him for anything or expected very much. But surely she had meant something more to him than just an hour's amusement!

Lights burned in the Rowe house which meant that Annie had the croup again. She could not bear the idea of going in to be greeted by her mother's complaints and her little sister's coughing.

She went on down the street past the straw piled before the cottages to deaden footsteps and allow the sick occupants to rest undisturbed, past the black crêpe swathed round the doors of those who had died. At the bottom the road curved round to the river in one direction and to the open gates of the mill in the other.

There was a light in the counting house window, and a saddled horse was tethered in the yard. Charles must have come down, as he often did, to check the books.

Emma went swiftly across the yard and gave the counting house door a little push. It yielded to the pressure of her knuckles and she mounted the steep wooden stairs. The room with its desk where old Ben Yarrow sat, its steel wall safe, its shelves stacked with bound ledgers was lit by a single oil-lamp. The tall, fair-haired man who bent over one of the ledgers turned at her footstep.

"Oh, it's you, Mr Edward!" Her voice was flat with disappointment.

"Were you looking for somebody, Emma?" he asked.

"For Saul," she invented quickly, coming further into the room.

"Isn't he at home?"

"I've been down by the river," she evaded, "taking a breath of air, and I saw the light on and I thought it might be Saul. I knew it wouldn't be Mr Charles because he's away courting at Holden Hall."

"I rather think we might be having a wedding in the family soon," Edward said pleasantly.

"Mr Charles and Miss Lumley, sir? That'll be grand, won't it?"

"Indeed it will," He glanced at her, deciding that certain suspicions he had entertained concerning his brother and Emma Rowe must be unfounded, for she sounded cheerfully interested. "If you like to sit down while I finish these I'll give you a pillion ride up to your mother's. Young girls ought not to wander about alone."

"Because of the French, sir?"

"I doubt if there are any French spies in this corner of the world," he said amused, "but there are always dangers."

"That's what makes life exciting, isn't it?" Emma said, but she sat down obediently, folding her hands primly, letting the shawl drop from her head and shoulders. It was warm and airless up here, the window closed tightly against any possible draught of air. Edward was in his shirt sleeves. In the glow of the lamp she could see the tiny golden hairs on his forearm. They reminded her of Charles and a little shiver ran along her nerves.

"How are you getting on at home?" he enquired, making a note at the side of the column of figures.

"Well enough, sir, but my mother gets low-spirited. I'll have to stay with her for a good long time, I reckon."

"I must call in," he said absently. "The trouble is, with so many sick to visit and so many funerals in the space of a month, my time seems not to be my own."

"And the books to do, sir?"

"Charles insists on my keeping an eye on things, as I have a share in the profits."

"It looks very clever, sir." She rose, leaving her shawl on the chair, and crossed to stand beside him.

"It's really very simple," he said, "That column shows what we pay out and this shows what we charge for the cloth and this is the difference between them which represents the profit we make. And this first column is broken down here in this ledger into freight charges, wages, maintainance of the looms and so on."

"It looks like a lot of money," Emma remarked.

"Not as much as you might think," he said wryly.

"Well it seems a lot to me." She smiled at him and he exclaimed, as he raised his own glance, "Why, you've been crying! What's the matter?"

"Nothing, Mr Edward." She would have turned aside, but he put his finger beneath her chin, tilting her head.

"Come now. You've been at Ladymoon for so long you seem like one of the family," he said kindly. "So what ails you?"

"It is because I feel it my duty to stay with my mother," she said, "and I want to come back to Ladymoon. When I'm in my mother's house I hardly ever see Mr Charles, or Miss Lucy, or — "

"Or what?"

"Or you, sir," she whispered. "Not seeing you hurts me more than the rest."

"Me!" He stared at her in astonishment.

"Yes, Mr Edward."

"My dear Emma, I am years older than you are," he stammered.

"Not so very many years," she said.

"I'm also a clergyman. A man of the cloth ought to control his natural desires until he weds. I confess to you that on occasion I have fallen from the path, but with you — "

"I'd not ask anything of you, sir," Emma murmured, "except that you'd be kind."

"Good Lord, lass! you're my mother's maid! You've been with us since you were

137

a child. I'd as soon think of loving my cousin Lucy!"

"I was thinking of need, sir, not love," Emma said. "You must have needs, like other men?"

She was looking at him with a gentle, questioning glance.

"Needs?" He stared back at her, while there rose in his mind memories of long, lonely hours wrestling with a sermon while in his thoughts danced forbidden visions of warm arms and a voice telling him he was wonderful.

He had always lacked his elder brother's dashing manner and handsome profile, but it had never made him jealous. He had never wanted to own the mill or the manor, and much of his energy had been devoted to the work and responsibilities of his growing parish. The thought of eventual marriage had lain at the back of his mind for years, but natural shyness had held him back and apart from the rare occasion when he and Charles had had a night on the town together, his desire for a mate had remained largely unassuaged and barely acknowledged.

"You're human, sir," Emma said in her newly gentle voice. "It must be powerful lonely all by yourself, working late into the night, riding for miles all over the countryside. I've often wished — "

"Wished what, my dear?"

"Wished that I were beautiful," she murmured.

"But you are!" Looking at her tumbling hair and the full breasts straining the thin wool of her dress, he wondered why he had only just realised that Emma Rowe was beautiful. "You are — most lovely."

"And loving too," she said, raising her hands to the laces that drew the bodice of her gown close about her throat.

"Emma, we must not," he said thickly, but she moved a step closer and said, "The knot is tangled, sir. Can you help?"

His fingers were cold and clumsy, fumbling with the lace, but the rest of him burned and throbbed without cessation. Under his hands the laces parted and the thin material slid down over plump white shoulders.

"You are truly beautiful," he tried to say, but the words broke from him in a kind of groan.

Emma stood still, her eyes closed, her lips parted in a little dreaming smile. If she didn't open her eyes it was so much easier to pretend that it was Mr Charles whose hands stripped her and whose mouth fastened on her breast.

Lucy was in her room. It was little altered

since the evening nine years before when she had first entered it. The clock with its silver fish stood on the dresser and the wardrobe held an array of gowns.

She had opened the casement, but there was no wind, no late chirping of birds settling into their nests, to lift the heavy stillness.

There was a pain between her eyes as if she had stared far too long at a very bright light. She sighed and went over to the window, leaning her elbows on the sill, peering into the darkness. Darkness as black as that she had seen all around Edward as he had flashed into her mind. She had not seen the kitchen or the dining dais at all, only Edward with the blackness creeping closer, beginning to cover his face.

She wished Saul would come and see her, for it was nearly a month since she had driven over to Clutterhouses and enjoyed that picnic on the grass. Neither she nor Aunt Trinity had been to Elisha Rowe's funeral for Charles had been adamant in his refusal to allow them to go into the village.

"Infections are spread by contact, so you'll oblige me by staying at home. I don't even want you to drive to church."

"You and Edward are in the Hollow and over at the church," Lucy had protested.

"Only because it's necessary," Charles had said. "And we scrub our hands thoroughly before we come into the house."

So she had kept to the house and garden, hoping that Saul might come. But he had not, and she consoled herself with the thought that he too feared to spread the infection. And he was doing well as temporary overseer. Charles had spoken highly of him. In a few months after the engagement had been made public, she would suggest that Saul approach Charles.

She had missed most of her supper, and now hunger gnawed at her. With any luck she'd find a piece of cold pie in the larder and a mug of buttermilk.

She put a loose robe over her petticoat and opened the door. The house was only fitfully lit by the lamps at the end of the corridor and at the turn in the stairs. She picked one up and padded down the staircase. Aunt Trinity, having probably exhausted herself in making suggestions for the wedding party, had obviously retired for the night. A thin line of light showed beneath the door of her bedroom.

There was another finger of light laid across the bottom of the library door. She guessed that Charles was there, lounging in one of the big leather chairs with a glass of madeira at his elbow. She wondered if he were imagining himself as the owner of Holden Hall, or if he dreamed of Sarah as she dreamed of Saul.

Edward had been a long time down at the counting house. She shivered, though the house was oppressively warm, and on impulse went through the parlour and opened the door of the little prayer room.

Lucy never went into the prayer room without feeling a sense of protection as if the very walls cradled her spirit. And she was abruptly in need of protection, though she could not have told why.

Setting the lamp on the table, she went over to where the cup stood and knelt down so that she and the moon-crowned woman were on the same level.

Only the face was engraved, but she knew, had always known, that the woman was tall and slender with blue wings that folded back, stretching further than human eye could see.

In the same way she knew that the cup had been brought to this place in the beginning by someone who loved it for its beauty and used it with reverence, and she knew that the power in the cup was very strong and became even stronger when certain people handled it.

142

She stared into the silver face and willed her mind to be still. Sometimes, if she looked for long enough, a kind of sleep came over her; not a real sleep, for she was always aware that she was Lucy Bostock of Ladymoon Manor. Yet another part of her seemed to walk in procession beneath a pylon gate into a high, white place with fine sand blown by a foreign wind.

And the incense, the music of the sistrum, the chanting, mingled in her mind until her troubles were of no importance.

Tonight her entire being remained firmly anchored to the ground. She clasped her hands together and spoke aloud, her voice beseeching.

"Lady! Lady, tell me what to do. Please tell me!"

Lightning streaked across the window and for an instant the face on the cup was ringed with flashes of blue light, and the twin serpents writhed and twisted. Thunder rumbled all about the eaves and the first drops of rain began to fall.

In the open doorway behind Lucy, Esther Evans backed away, her hands over her mouth, her eyes terrified. She was not supposed to be in this part of the manor at all, but she occasionally took the risk of sneaking from the kitchen. It was not that she meant any harm but the house was full of such pretty things. There were embroidered screens in the parlour, and delicate crystal vases, and pictures in silver frames. She liked to look at them with her thin fingers. The golden cup was the most beautiful thing of all, but for some reason she had not wanted to touch it.

Lightning flashed again and she ran barefoot through the parlour into the narrow main hall. The door was on the latch in readiness for Edward's return, and as Esther paused to catch her breath, it swung open and he appeared on the threshold, rain lashing his head and shoulders.

"Mr Edward." She bobbed a curtsey, hoping he would not ask her why she was up so late.

But he looked at her vaguely, and his voice was so slurred that for a moment she thought he had been drinking.

"Is my brother at home?"

"In the library, sir. Shall I take your cloak?"

"Call Charles," he instructed. "I am — not well, Esther. Charles had better help me to my room."

He had not been drinking. She had seen the high, burning cheekbones and blurred eyes of a fever victim before. Even as she watched he retched suddenly and doubled over in pain.

There was a pattering of feet across the parlour and Lucy stood there, staring at her cousin. She had clutched her robe about her small frame, and all she said in a dry, hopeless little voice was,

"I saw it, Esther. I saw it."

Part Two

5

1810

"If only Edward could have been present." Trinity dabbed her eyes with a black-bordered handkerchief. "These past six months have been so sad for us all, and yet we cannot mourn for ever. But I confess I do not enjoy the notion of entertaining."

"Only Mr Lumley and his daughter are coming to supper!" Lucy exclaimed. "You can scarcely call that entertaining."

"But we are to go down to the mill to drink the healths of Charles and Sarah," Trinity fretted. "If I begin to think of poor, dear Edward — "

"Then we don't think of him," Lucy said firmly, patting her aunt's cap into position. "Charles and Sarah have already delayed their engagement a further three months. We owe it to them to be cheerful and to look to the future."

"An August wedding will be charming," Trinity agreed, "and I think it will be permissible to come out of mourning completely by then. As you so rightly say, we cannot grieve for ever."

"I think I hear them." Lucy cast a hasty glance at her own grey-gowned figure and hurried down the stairs.

Charles, flushed and handsome after his ride, was ushering in the visitors. In the background Esther waited to receive the outdoor garments. She looked, Lucy thought fleetingly, very different from the ragged girl she had seen on the moors the previous year. Esther's hair was wound neatly at the back of her head and she wore an attractive gown in a soft shade of rust. Cook declared she was a good, willing girl who never minded working long hours and never asked for afternoons off. Lucy had enquired if Esther would like to be parlourmaid, but the other had shook her head and for an instant fear had flashed into her eyes.

"Miss Lucy, you look very charming," Daniel Lumley said, bowing over her hand.

She smiled up at him in the frank, confiding manner that he often wished his own beloved Sarah would display.

"My aunt will be down soon. Won't you come into the parlour?"

She led the way into the room where sherry, port and small cakes were laid ready. As always Lucy felt insignificant next to her cousin's fiancee. Sarah, who could not be expected to confine herself to mourning, had achieved a tactful compromise in a gown of deep lavender, her hair hidden beneath one of the fashionable new turbans in a paler shade. On her left hand gleamed the single, flawless diamond she had requested. It was clear that Charles admired her greatly. It was also clear that she allowed him no familiarities at all, but treated him with cool amusement. Lucy wondered, as she passed round the refreshments, if Sarah Lumley would have agreed to marry him at all if she had not failed to catch a husband with a title.

"Trinity, my dear." Daniel rose as she came in. "I am pleased to see you so recovered."

"One must bear up," she murmured, her eyes filling up again.

"Mrs Holden." Sarah bowed her head coolly, avoiding Trinity's affectionate embrace.

"You look lovely," Trinity said warmly. "Is that the new style of bonnet? It's vastly becoming, my dear. I must take a trip to York one of these days and see if I cannot find something similar for Lucy and myself. Was your journey a tolerably comfortable one?"

She spoke as if untold dangers were to be found between Ladymoon Manor and

151

Holden Hall. Yet as a girl she had braved a long voyage across the Atlantic.

"Very comfortable. Even my old bones were not too much shaken."

"We have given Sarah the guest-room next to Lucy," Trinity said. "You will not object to sleeping in Edward's room, Daniel? His possessions have all been removed. We have to be sensible about these things."

"To remember the dead with love but not to build mausoleums," Daniel said. "We'll be very happy where ever you put us, and when the wedding is celebrated I hope very much that you and your niece will stay at Holden Hall."

"Thank you." Trinity's face dropped slightly. She had never liked the big gloomy house and had always been pleased that her husband had not inherited it."

"I'd like to see my room," Sarah said.

"I'll come up with you." Lucy rose and led the way to the inner hall. The other followed more slowly, looking about her with faint criticism in her face.

"Are there no other stairs?," she enquired.

"There's a very narrow flight built into the thickness of the wall behind the parlour chimney, but they only lead up to Aunt Trinity's room, so nobody bothers to use them these days," Lucy explained. "This main staircase divides to left and right and then twists to left and right and then twists round again to the upper corridor. The house was built on different levels and added to later on."

"It's not as large as I expected," Sarah said. "You know, I believe I visited here occasionally when I was a child, but everything seems larger when one is small. I suppose Mrs Holden will move into the guest room when Charles and I are married."

"I suppose she might." Lucy opened the door of the red room and ushered Sarah within.

"It would be more practical. Edward's and Charles's old rooms would then be suitable for nurseries."

"I suppose so." Lucy watched in astonishment as the other went over to the window, fingering the ruby velvet curtains.

"These are old," she said over her shoulder. "The material is rubbed in places. Mrs Holden will prefer a more modern design."

"She might," Lucy said coldly.

She was beginning to hope that her cousin and his bride would spend most of their time at Holden Hall.

"Charles said we were to drive down to the mill before supper," Sarah said.

"The millhands will want to drink your health."

"Is there anywhere I could wash my hands?"

"Wash? Oh, we have an indoor closet now," Lucy said proudly, "When I first came here we went out back, but the little sewing room has been converted. I'll show you where it is."

"The house is so cramped that I'm sure I can locate it," Sarah said.

Either something had occurred to put her out of temper or she was even more disagreeable than Lucy remembered.

The younger girl pulled a face at the other's retreating back and went downstairs again where her aunt and Daniel Lumley were chatting with the eagerness of old friends who seldom meet.

It was dusk when they took their places in the Lumley coach. The servants, barring Cook who remained to give last minute touches to the supper, were to follow in the pony-trap.

It was a fine, warm evening with no more than the faintest of breezes. March was coming in like a lamb. The dusk softened the outlines of mill and cottages, blurring the reality of sagging gates and cracked window panes. Charles declared with prices so high

154

and production lagging, he could not possibly afford to undertake expensive repairs. But Sarah had her diamond ring for all that.

The mill gates were open and trestle tables held hams, cheeses, bread, fruit tarts, and flagons of ale. Charles had paid for those at least, and on the actual wedding day there would be a similar feast with a new shilling for every man, woman and child.

The yard was already crowded, and a ragged cheer went up as Trinity stepped down. She had always been popular in the Hollow even though she seldom went there, but the grief she still nursed for her husband and the more recent death of her son caused most people to regard her with sympathy.

Lucy looked round eagerly for any sign of Saul. The fever abated and the dead, including Edward, laid to rest, Saul had resumed his Sunday afternoon rides with her. Not every Sunday, for bad weather often made their meetings impractical. He had not yet come to the house as a formal suitor, nor even spoken of his feelings but Lucy was as sure of them as she was of her own. Now, not having seen him in a fortnight, she looked about eagerly. There was, however, no sign of any of the Rowes.

"Friends, many of you know Mr Lumley who is about to complete his first year of

155

office as a member of the Council." Charles had mounted a chair and raised his voice.

"Aye, but it's Lumley's lass you brought to show us," someone called.

"And here she is! I present my fiancee, Miss Sarah Lumley, who in August will become the new Mrs Holden." Charles held out his hand to Sarah who, emerged from the coach, stood stiffly next to her father.

There was another round of applause and one small boy, carried away by the occasion, flung his cap into the air, shouting, "Long live the king and Wellington!"

"Long may we all live!" Charles seized a tankard from the table and held it aloft. "My friends, I ask you to drink to my happiness and to your own."

There were murmurs of "Hear! Hear!" as the toast was drunk. Lucy, sipping the bitter ale, found it impossible to blame Sarah who, miserably ill-at-ease, barely touched her lips to the froth of her own tankard.

"Are you biding a while, master?" Tom Turley asked respectfully. "You'd be right and welcome."

"A few minutes only, for I'll not keep you from your supper." Charles stepped down and, taking Sarah's hand, began to lead her from group to group. He was pleased by the reception accorded them, but a trifle disappointed at Sarah's own reaction. She was too sheltered at Holden Hall, he decided, and ought to be encouraged to mingle more with other people.

"Is it true there's to be laying offs in the summer?" someone was enquiring.

He frowned slightly, bending a reproachful glance upon the speaker. Will Beeston was a Methodist and a man who would enjoy introducing a discordant note into the proceedings.

"I've no intention of laying off good workers," Charles said at last.

"That wasn't what I asked, master," Beeston said. "Will there be any lay offs at all?"

"I cannot say. Summer's not yet come."

"But new looms have to be ordered months ahead," Beeston persisted.

"I'm hoping we can keep pace with orders without having to buy any. Work well and there's no need to fear." Charles nodded pleasantly and moved on to talk with Peter Grinstead who had recently been taken on as a clerk and could be relied on to steer the conversation into less troubled waters.

The ale was circulating again and people were beginning to help themselves to the provisions on the table. Someone at the back of the crowd struck up a tune on a fiddle and

157

a few of the young ones were pairing off for a round dance. Flares had been kindled and in their light the faces of the people were illuminated, their shadows exaggerated into grotesque shapes that leaped and dipped over the cobbles.

Lucy caught sight of Joan Rowe and beckoned to her. She fancied that the girl came reluctantly, but it might have been shyness. Apart from Emma, she was not well acquainted with Saul's younger brothers and sisters. This one had the family's dark eyes and hair and her dress was neat, but she scuffed her toe back and forth on the cobbles with a little rasping sound.

"It's Joan, isn't it? Are the rest of the family not here?"

"No, miss."

"Nobody is sick, I hope?"

"No, miss."

"Are they coming later then?"

"I don't know, miss." Joan hung her head, twisting her fingers in her skirt.

"Lucy, my dear, we're going back to the house now. Cook will be very cross if supper is spoiled."

Aunt Trinity was speaking to her. Lucy turned to answer but when she glanced back again Joan had slipped away.

"I was wondering where Saul Rowe was,"

Lucy said. "None of the Rowes are here, except Joan, and now she's gone."

"He probably has business elsewhere," Trinity said vaguely. "Are you all right, Sarah? You look a little pale."

"I have a slight headache," Sarah said. She still had a slightly disagreeable look on her face.

At her side Charles said, his voice hearty, "Sarah will have to accustom herself to an occasional evening of gaiety. We have all been penned up for too long."

"I was not aware that rubbing shoulders with rustics constituted an evening's gaiety," Sarah said lightly.

"I think we can do better than that," Charles said, handing her into the coach. "Mr Lumley, I have it in mind to give a larger party for my beautiful bride, and to open up Ladymoon Manor and invite some of our neighbours. Not that we are overwhelmed with them at the best of times."

"London was much gayer," Sarah said, sinking into the corner with pouting underlip.

"We'll visit London when we're wed," Charles said.

"I shall think about it." She shot him a provoking glance out of her narrow eyes.

"So pleasant to see everybody so happy," said Trinity. "I must come down to the

Hollow more frequently. I shall be pleased when the new minister is appointed, not that anyone could take dear Edward's place, but with no services being held at the church and no parish visiting by a minister, I do feel a mite uneasy. So much sedition about!"

"Not at Holden Mill," Charles said. "My workers know that I treat them fairly."

"Spoil them," Sarah commented. "It would increase your profits if you installed new looms, wouldn't it? I heard you talking to that man, Charles, as if you owed him some explanation for what you did with your own business."

"These are independent folk, and most of them have lost relatives in the fever," Trinity said gently. "They need to feel their jobs are secure, and they demand the right to speak their minds."

"Sarah would have all the servants as bondsmen or slaves," Daniel said.

His daughter bit her lip and sighed resentfully. Sometimes she thought her father took a malicious pleasure in mentioning slaves as if to remind her that her own grandmother had been one.

"I think it might be wise to have another discussion about those looms," she said loudly.

"Surely you will be too busy choosing

material for all the new curtains you intend buying," Lucy said sweetly.

"I shall go to London for those," Sarah returned with equal sweetness. "Charles, you would not object if we took your cousin with us to London? It would benefit her greatly."

They were near the Rowe house. Lucy, ignoring Sarah, looked towards it as the coach rounded the corner and lumbered onto the open moor above the river.

There had been no lights in the windows but Charles, as if influenced by some thought of hers, said, "I wonder that Saul wasn't there. As overseer it was his place to join in the celebrations."

"Perhaps he thought we were going to stay longer," Trinity said, "but as Sarah has a headache — oh, there is Saul, and Emma with him!"

"Come to make their explanations and excuses, I trust." Charles opened the coach door and stepped down.

"Mr Charles, I'd like a private word with you," Saul said, coming forward.

His voice was pitched higher than usual, and his face, seen in the flickering light of the coach lamps, was set in lines of firm resolution. Lucy, climbing down, felt her first impulse of relief die away. Saul neither

161

looked at her nor spoke, but faced Charles squarely, his arm about Emma who seemed to shrink against him.

"Is it absolutely essential at this moment?" Charles asked. "We are about to go into supper."

"It's essential," Saul said briefly.

"If you'd care to go into the house," Charles said, turning to the others, "I'll be with you in a moment."

Sarah was pausing, her eyes darting from one to the other.

"What is it?" she demanded. "Why do you allow this man to interrupt us?"

"The name is Saul Rowe, Miss Lumley," Saul said. "I'm overseer to Mr Charles."

"Then save your business for working hours," she said sharply.

"This is a private matter, not to do with the mill," Saul said. "We hoped to catch you before you went down to the Hollow, but you'd left when we got here."

"You'd better come in then," Charles said irritably. "Mr Lumley, this ought not to take very long. If you would like to join the others at the table, I'll be with you very soon."

"I think he ought to stay," Emma said in a loud shaking voice. "I think they all should stay!"

Trinity, gazing at them, said, with a

162

bewildered flutter of her plump white hands, "Then you'd better all come into the parlour. I really cannot understand what is going on, and I shall insist on knowing all about it."

"I hoped to keep all of it private," Saul said, but he followed the others, his arm still around his sister. Cook had cleared away the empty glasses and built up the fire. The apartment looked warm and comfortable, its windows shuttered against the night.

Trinity sat down in her usual chair and motioned the Lumleys to the couch. Lucy sat on the arm of her aunt's chair, watching Saul and Emma as they came in. She wished that Saul would look at her, but he kept his eyes fixed on Charles.

Her own eyes moved to Emma. It was weeks since she had seen the girl and now, looking at her, she felt a sense of shock. Emma's rosiness had fled and there were dark shadows beneath her eyes. She was wrapped in a voluminous cloak, her hair plaited tightly under a neat white cap.

"Well, get on with it then!" Charles said in sudden impatience.

"I wished it to be private," said Saul. "It was not my intention to shame you before your guests."

"Shame! What shame?" Charles demanded.

163

"That which matches my shame," Emma said.

She was opening her cloak and even before its folds were swept aside Lucy knew. She clenched her fists against the cry of outrage that broke from Sarah.

"Charles! How dare this woman force her way in here? I demand some explanation of her condition immediately."

"Isn't it plain enough for you to grasp, miss?" Emma retorted, her mouth twisting into mockery.

"Charles, you had best explain," Trinity said in a low voice.

"I am as puzzled as you are," Charles said. "I haven't the faintest idea what she is babbling about."

"She is obviously with child," Daniel said, his voice carefully controlled. "I suggest we begin at the beginning and enquire who fathered it."

"It was the master," Emma said. "I didn't want to tell, Mr Charles, but Saul made me."

"She hid her state from us all until now," Saul said heavily. "We never guessed for she's been wearing loose smocks, but my mother noticed and I got the truth of it. She's six months gone with child."

"Then it's not mine. Emma left here seven

164

months back, and I've not spoken to her more than once since then."

"Once was sufficient," Emma cried reproachfully. "I know the very day just as you do. You'd been over to Holden Hall to ask Miss Lumley to marry you, and I waited for you as you'd bade me wait. You told me your marriage would make no difference to us, for we could still meet. Oh, Mr Charles, you acted so loving."

"All this is fantasy," Charles said.

"And the next day we heard Mr Edward had been taken bad with the fever, and he died. And we've not met since, it's true, for I feared to tell you how it was with me, not wishing to spoil your chance of being master of Hall!"

"You swore to me you had no entanglements," Daniel said.

"Nor had I, sir!" Charles cried, his face scarlet. "I spoke the truth."

"But what of past affairs? Had you already seduced this girl?"

"I may have — paid her compliments, teased her a little."

"It was more than that," Emma said, beginning to cry. "He told me that no harm would come from his loving me. I loved him back, sir, and I'm to blame for that, but he said he loved me and would

165

never let marriage come between us."

"She lies," Charles said.

"But you did meet her on the night Edward was taken sick," Trinity said, wrinkling her brow. "I recall you saying something of it at the supper table."

"I met her by chance out on the moor," Charles said. "She was waiting for me, but I'd not told her to wait. When I saw her, I took the opportunity of informing her that it was over between us. It had been over anyway since she returned to her mother's."

"You said that what lay between us was too strong ever to be ended," Emma sobbed.

"These are vicious lies. She is twisting everything that took place into some tale of her own," Charles said.

"Perhaps she took up with one of the village lads," Trinity suggested.

"She's no sweetheart in the Hollow," objected Saul. "If she'd been walking out with anyone I'd have heard of it."

"She could have met him secretly," Charles said.

"As you and I used to meet, Mr Charles?" Emma dabbed her eyes with the edge of her cloak. "After you'd had me, sir, do you think I'd look at a village lad? It was you I loved, and I'd not have brought trouble on you, but Saul made me tell."

166

"Have you any proof at all of what you say, my dear?" Daniel asked. "I think we can accept the fact that some kind of relationship existed between Charles and yourself in the past, but you say yourself you met only the one time since. And it's your word against his that anything happened between you then."

"He told me to be patient and wait," Emma said. "He told me we'd not see each other for a while, but that I was to stay true and not walk out with anybody else. He said he'd send me ten shillings a week. I was to collect it from old Ben down at the counting house on Fridays. I've been collecting it every week, sir. I used to slip in when Saul wasn't around."

"You'll not find any ten shilling payments entered on any ledger," Charles began.

"I wouldn't know about that, sir," Emma said. "I only know I kept all the money. I've thirteen pounds, sewn into my mattress. I never spent any of it."

"You could have got that money from someone else," Trinity said.

"But I didn't, Mrs Holden. Old Ben will remember giving it to me, even if there's nothing written down."

"All right, all right!" Charles rose in agitation. "I did give her ten shillings a week. I was sorry for the girl. She wanted

167

to come back here and she was threatening to make herself a nuisance. So I gave her ten shillings a week."

"A skilled weaver doesn't earn more than seven!" Saul exclaimed.

"It was to keep her quiet," Charles muttered.

"But that cannot have been necessary," Daniel objected. "If the affair was over then there was little point in her talking about it, even to me. You were well aware that I hadn't expected you to live like a saint."

"Perhaps it was to help with the poor baby," Trinity said.

"But the child cannot have been aware that she was pregnant when the payments began," Daniel pointed out.

"It was a retaining fee," Emma murmured. "You said you wished to retain me for the future. I didn't want to be paid, sir, but you said it would ease your mind to know I had something of my own. You said the payments would only stop if I walked out with anybody else."

"Oh, Charles, how could you?" Trinity reproached.

"Hell's teeth! How often do I have to tell you the bitch is lying?" Charles ground out.

"You'll not speak of my sister in those terms," Saul said coldly.

168

"How else can I?" Charles demanded. "She has turned everything around. Cannot you see there is nothing but malice behind this? She waits for six months, hiding her condition, and on the very day my engagement is made public she comes here to make trouble."

"I never wanted to come," Emma said. "I never would have told, sir, but Saul was so angry. He forced me to come, but you'd already left for the Hollow."

"I wanted to keep it private between us," Saul said. "It's never been my intention to cause any trouble, for you've been a fair employer. But Emma is carrying your child, Mr Charles, and I expect you to do the honourable thing."

"What had you in mind?" Daniel asked.

"Marriage, sir. Emma's a good lass, for all that she was foolish enough to listen to Mr Charles's pretty words. But he was older than she and knew very well what he was about."

"You must be out of your mind," Charles said, "If you really think I'd ever marry Emma."

"I never asked for that," Emma said. "I knew you wanted Holden Hall, but you told me often and often that you cared nothing for Miss Lumley and would never cease from desiring me."

169

Sarah, who had sat in frozen silence, rose, her face full of contempt.

"Father, is it necessary to subject me to any more of this filth?" she asked.

"My dear, we must remain very calm," Trinity said. "We must decide what is best to do and then do it. You cannot allow a previous — relationship to spoil what you have."

"What my daughter has," said Daniel, "is the certainty of inheriting a large estate."

"That was not my first consideration," Charles said.

"But it loomed large in your thinking when you paid suit to her. You admitted as much."

"I was honest with you, Mr Lumley."

"But not with my sister," Saul interposed.

"Nor with me. I told you that I'd not stand for any scandal," Daniel said. "You gave your solemn word, and then you went straight out and met this young woman."

"By chance! I met her by chance, damn it!"

"She was waiting for you."

"I knew nothing about it!" Charles shouted. "Nothing happened between us on that occasion."

"You arranged to pay her a regular and generous allowance."

"I was sorry for her."

"And now, six months later, she is six months gone with child."

"Not my child! Sarah, you must believe that!" He swung round upon her, his hand outstretched, but she evaded him, her face like stone.

"I would like to go back to Holden Hall now, father," she said.

"But you haven't had your supper yet!" Trinity cried in distress. "At least stay and have your supper!"

"I'm not hungry, and my head is splitting. Will you please tell one of your servants to be so good as to bring down my bag? I've not unpacked anything, so we can be on our way at once."

"But the engagement?"

"There is no engagement," Sarah said. "You may consider yourself free from any promise you ever made to me, as I shall."

"This is ridiculous!" Charles cried angrily. "We cannot throw away an entire future on the word of a lying slut!"

"You may be master, Mr Charles," Saul said, "but that gives you no right to call Emma such names! She lived here in a manner of speaking under your protection. You took advantage of her, and she has a right to be married."

171

"But not to me! I'm hardly likely to ally myself with the sister of one of my own workers."

"You should, at the very least, make provision for the baby," Trinity reproached.

"I would, if it were my child. I'll not be pressed into acknowledging someone else's hedge-get."

"It makes no matter," said Sarah, "Are you coming, father, or do I have to drive home alone?"

"I'm coming, my dear." Daniel rose, leaning heavily on his ivory-topped cane.

"Daniel, please!" Trinity caught at his arm. "We must talk about this. Some kind of arrangement can surely be made."

"I'll not entrust my daughter into the care of a man who has no honour," Daniel said. "You'll forgive my bluntness, my dear. I have always had a deep affection for you and your husband was a fine man. But I cannot stand by and see my daughter marry a man who seduces a servant and is not man enough to acknowledge his child. I'm truly sorry, my dear."

He bowed and went out, Sarah at his heels. The others stood or sat in silence, listening to Daniel's voice in the hall beyond.

"If you please, Mrs Holden, I'm to put the bags in the coach again?" Esther came in, her eyes inquisitive.

Trinity nodded mutely.

"This is intolerable!" Charles exclaimed. "We cannot possibly let it end like this. Sarah is pledged to me, and I'll hold her to that!"

"You cannot! She has every right to change her mind," Trinity said.

Esther came through with the two monogrammed cases. Her eyes were downcast now, and she went past into the outer hall with her head bent. A moment later the sound of the departing coach came to their ears.

Lucy had said nothing. She sat on the arm of her aunt's chair, her green eyes moving from one to the other, her icy hands clasped so tightly that the knuckles showed white. She was so cold that she couldn't remember what it was like to be warm.

"They've gone." Trinity made a helpless little gesture. "Oh, my dear, I am so sorry. One might have expected a little more understanding, but I always thought her a cold young woman!"

"She never could have loved you as I love you," Emma said.

"Love? You'd do well not to use that word," Charles said. "I don't blame you, Saul, for you believe her tale and have the right to speak on her behalf, for she's your sister. But she's lying. And I'll not be threatened or bullied into acknowledging any bastard she bears. So you may take yourselves off home, and be damned to you both."

He turned on his heel and walked through to the library, slamming the door behind him.

"You had best leave," Trinity said. "I am very sorry, but I cannot bear any more just now."

She rested her head on her hand, sighing deeply. It had been a strain for her to go down to the Hollow, for it held memories of happier times when she had driven down to the counting house with her two small sons. Edward had been so good and quiet. Charles had been the mischievous one, forever wanting to take the reins of the trap, asking questions, never still. Matthew had been so proud of his sons, and now he and Edward were dead and Charles was accused of dishonour.

She looked round for Lucy but her niece had left the parlour.

Lucy caught up with Saul and Emma just beyond the outhouses. She was panting a little for she had run fast and embarrassment made her stammer a little.

"W — wait. Please! I — I cannot see you

174

both leave in such anger."

"Not with you," Saul said. "This is none of your doing."

"Then you must allow me to help in some way," Lucy pleaded. "Emma, you will require things for the babe. And you ought not to work too hard."

"I can manage very well," Emma said stiffly.

"I'll bring you some things," Lucy began, but Saul interrupted,

"My mother swears she'll not have one of your family in her home unless Emma is respectably wed."

"Then I'll send Esther. Please, Saul, don't refuse. Esther can come to help out."

"That's kind of you," Saul said, his eyes and voice softening.

"I'll send her over tomorrow. I'm sure — my cousin will come to some arrangement."

"That's as maybe," Saul said. "We'll not lower ourselves to beg."

He put his arm round his sister and urged her forward again.

Lucy stood irresolute, her mouth open to call them back. But there was nothing else she could think of to say.

6

Summer gilded the landscape. After the promise of spring the fruits of August seemed even larger and more luxuriant. The harvest was early and the light rain of the previous day had brightened the grass and plumped the river.

Lucy's green dress and straw bonnet matched the mood of the afternoon. She looked particularly charming in green for it intensified her brilliant eyes and softened her red curls. The trap had recently been painted and gleamed honey bright. On the seat was a basket containing some baby garments that Trinity had knitted and a jar of strawberry preserves. She was safe enough in taking them to the Rowe house for Charles was in York and not likely to return until the morrow. He was very much opposed to any visits she made to see Emma or the baby, although he made no objection to the rides she still occasionally took with Saul.

The Rowe house looked somewhat improved since Saul had repainted door and window frames and bullied his two young brothers into weeding the garden, but even with his increased wage as overseer Lucy knew that he found it difficult to manage. Charles had stopped the ten shilling payments, and refused to have Emma or the child mentioned. Yet there was no possible doubt that it was a Holden.

Lucy, climbing down and heaving down the basket, paused to look into the wooden cradle that had been put out in the sunshine with a fringed canopy over it. In the shade of that Tabitha lay gurgling, her round face framed in a white bonnet. At two months she was enchanting, her fair curls peeping from under the white brim, her blue eyes beginning to recognise those who bent above her.

"Who's a bonny little lass then?" Lucy put her finger into the minute palm and smiled as the plump fingers curved about it. A little shiver of envy and delight ran through her. It would be so marvellous to have a baby of her own, and this one, though unacknowledged, was only her niece.

"Good afternoon, Miss Lucy." Esther, her hair scraped under a kerchief and an apron over her dimity gown, came to the open door.

"Cleaning on your day off? I thought you'd be away on the moors or down by the river," Lucy said.

177

"Emma asked me to come. It's all right isn't it? I'll be back in time for supper, miss."

"It's perfectly alright. But Emma is surely recovered enough to do her own work."

"Mrs Anna's not so grand today," Esther said excusingly. "She says she's not happy down at the mill. She never could abide the chatter of the other women, and it makes it harder for her when she's widow of the last overseer and mother of the present one."

"She was lucky to be taken back at all," Lucy said, coldness creeping into her voice. "Profits are down and prices so high that Mr Charles has been forced to raise wages as it is. You are not to let them take advantage of your good nature, Esther."

"No, miss." Esther moved aside as Lucy went past. The girl always did that, avoiding any physical contact with her young mistress.

The main living room looked clean and bright, but the two faces turned towards her were faintly hostile. Probably both Emma and her mother had heard Lucy's comments beyond the door.

Anna Rowe did look drawn and pale. At her side Emma seemed to bloom like a dark rose in contrast. She was wearing a red dress, its narrow skirt flounced, and her hair was piled up in a chignon.

178

"I brought some clothes for Tabitha." Lucy set the basket on the table and nodded pleasantly.

"Very kind of you, Miss Lucy," Anna said stiffly.

"Esther says you're not feeling well." She looked at Anna who dropped her eyes and said. "It's this pain that frets me. Like a knife twisting in me."

"Then you ought to see a doctor. Cannot Saul take you into York?"

"So that I end up dead on an operating table like young Johnny Turley? Thank you, miss, but I'll not bother."

"I could ask the doctor to look in on you if you like," Lucy offered. "It'd be no trouble."

"When your cousin shamed my lass I swore I'd never have a Holden over my doorstep again," Anna said. "Well, you were so good, lending Esther to help out and taking an interest in the babe that I changed my mind and let you come. But I'll not stand for interference, Miss Lucy."

"Though you don't object to using my maid to do the cleaning your own daughters could do," Lucy said sharply.

"If I'd my rights I'd be Mrs Holden of Ladymoon Manor now," Emma said, "and Esther would be working for me."

"What of Joan and Mary? They're big girls, big enough to help out."

"They went down to catch a bit of fish for our supper," Anna said. "We cannot run to meat every day like rich folks."

"You should keep them closer to home," Lucy said. "Tell Esther to bring the basket with her when she comes back to the manor tonight. Good-day."

She went out with her head high and a scowl on her face. It was a little hard that her friendliness should be resented, and galling to see Emma put on airs as if she were a deeply wronged woman. She'd always had a name in the Hollow for being flighty. Yet there was no denying that Tabitha with her blue eyes and fair hair was the image of Charles.

Her ill-temper evaporated as she beheld Saul, striding towards her with a gun over his shoulder. The added responsibilities of his job had given him more authority in his bearing. He was no longer a boy but a confident man.

"I've been visiting my niece," she said, as he came up to her. "She's a beautiful child."

"Aye, a good one too, for she never cries."

"But your mother is not well. She ought to see a doctor about the pain she has."

180

"She'll not be told." His glance went past her to where Esther bent over the cradle.

"I hoped we might take a ride later," Lucy said. "It's more than a month since we went to Romany Crag."

"I went out to see if I could shoot something for the larder but the word must have got out," he said ruefully, "for every bird and beast went to ground. If I'd have known earlier you required me — "

"It's not a question of 'required', Saul," she said, a little hurt. "I thought it would be pleasant to ride together, that's all. You could always invite me."

"I'll not come to Ladymoon Manor," he said. "Not until your cousin makes an honest woman of my sister."

"But that's foolish. You talk to Charles at the mill!"

"Only in the way of business," he said stubbornly. "We never speak of personal matters."

"Then why not come to the manor?"

"Because it wouldn't be fitting."

"I come to your house," she argued.

"It's kind of you, and Emma is grateful though she might not say much."

"I don't do it to be kind," she said. "I do it for all our sakes, Saul. Don't you understand that? Bitterness is such an evil

181

thing, and affection so important."

"Self-respect is important too," Saul said. He was helping her up to the seat of the trap. She held his hand for a moment longer, trying to read the expression in his tanned face.

"Saul? Things are not wrong between us, are they?" she ventured.

"You are not to blame for what Mr Charles has done," he said.

"I didn't mean — oh, never mind." She withdrew her own hand, waved to Esther, and drove back up the hill. Her cheerful mood had evaporated and she felt uneasy and frustrated.

It was, she decided, too warm to remain out of doors. Already her skin was beginning to prickle. She went into the parlour but Aunt Trinity was evidently lying down for the apartment was empty of bits of unfinished embroidery and half empty boxes of chocolates.

From the library across the hall Charles called, "Lucy? Is that you?"

"I thought you still in York." She hurried into the wide apartment where her cousin sat.

"I got short shift there," he said moodily, glancing up from the depths of the chair in which he was sunk. "Daniel Lumley was at the Rose and Crown, talking business with a mob of aldermen. The air froze when I walked in."

"He didn't insult you, did he?"

"He bowed and enquired after the health of my mother and cousin," Charles said. "I enquired after the health of his daughter. 'Oh', said he, 'Sarah has gone down to London to stay with friends for an indefinite period'. And then he turned his back and went on discussing repairs to the town wall."

"I'm very sorry," Lucy said awkwardly. "I'm truly sorry."

"I was too much of a gentleman to enquire if she went off still wearing the diamond ring I'd bought for her," he said. "Pour me a drink, Lucy. A stiff one if you please."

"You have been drinking a lot recently," she said, obeying.

"And wenching too, over in the York stews. Are you presuming to lecture me on that?"

"I worry about you, cousin."

"Kind Lucy!" He had evidently drunk a considerable amount already, for his blue eyes were slightly blurred, his face flushed with more than the ride.

"I went to see the baby," she said cautiously.

183

"Which one? There are dozens of them crawling about in the Hollow."

"You know very well which one I mean!" Lucy said crossly. "Charles, she is such a pretty little thing. Blue eyes and fair hair and a smile just like Aunt Trinity's. I wish you would — "

"Acknowledge her as my darling little bastard daughter? Marry her slut of a mother?" he interrupted.

"Emma is not so bad. You must have liked her once."

"She amused me, but all that finished when I became engaged to Sarah. She'll not foist her hedge-get on me now."

"At least give something for the child's support."

"Nay, I'll not be caught in that snare!" he exclaimed. "Let's drop the subject. Is that a new gown? It's vastly becoming."

"It's an old one and you've seen it before."

"Well, it suits you. You're a pretty thing, cousin. A very pretty thing."

The timbre of his voice had altered and he was looking at her in an oddly considering fashion.

"How old are you now?" he enquired abruptly.

"I was twenty in March. Nobody," said Lucy, "ever remembers.

184

"And not walking out with anybody."

"Not walking out with anybody."

"Twenty years old and heartfree," he mused. "And I am near forty and cannot have the woman I want. She will not return from London until she is wed. You may depend upon that. No doubt he'll buy her a bigger diamond, and her father will rejoice that Holden Hall is to pass to an honourable man. Well, I think you and I could clip the edges of their satisfaction."

"How?" she asked.

"We could be married," he said. "Oh you have no fortune but that would make the insult keener. People would never be quite sure if I had jilted her for your sake or if she had jilted me."

"Marriage! But you don't love me," Lucy said.

"I didn't *love* Sarah either," he pointed out. "In fact this emotion of love, if it exists, seems to have passed me by, but I am exceedingly fond of you and you are heartfree."

She wanted to cry out that she wasn't so, that she loved Saul who was only biding his time until he could ask for her hand, but she could only stand frozen, her eyes fixed on Charles.

"My mother would be pleased," he

continued. "A whole new generation of Holdens to live at Ladymoon Manor!"

"We're cousins. I don't think marriage between cousins is wise," she stammered.

"Much you know about breeding," he said in amusement. "If both parents are healthy it strengthens the stock. Now you and I have never had a day's illness in our lives. We'd match well together."

"It's out of the question," she said. "To marry me so that you can spite Sarah Lumley! I never heard anything so immoral!"

"I'll not force you to it," he said, "but I urge you to consider it."

"I intend to put it right out of my mind," she declared. "You must be in your cups to think of such a thing!"

"I am fond of you," he began, but she shook her head.

"Please, Charles! I'll not wed you and I'll not listen to any more arguments. You may drop the subject and we'll not mention it again."

She was afraid he might prevent her from leaving the room, but he remained in his chair, sipping the brandy and made no move to intercept her as she went out.

The proposal had been so unexpected that she was not certain whether to lose her temper or to laugh. Charles, she decided, must be out of his senses if he imagined she'd agree to wed him in order to salve his wounded pride. It was as much an insult to her as he hoped it would be to Sarah Lumley, and when he was in a more sober mood she'd point out the fact. On second thoughts it would be wiser to forget the entire episode.

She had just reached that conclusion when footsteps and agitated voices sounded in the hall. This was definitely not going to be a peaceful afternoon.

In the hall Cook and Jessie were talking to Esther and Joan Rowe. Lucy could hear only a babble of disconnected phrases but, as she arrived on the threshold of the parlour, Joan called out, forsaking her carefully polite English for the thick local dialect, "'Tis our Mary, miss, int beck! Drowned dead!"

"What!" The colour drained from Lucy's face.

"Esther! What is it? What's happened?"

"It's true, miss," Esther said. "Mary fell into the river. It's deep where they were fishing, and she slipped down the bank. Joan couldn't reach her, so she ran for help."

"They pulled her," Joan sobbed, "but she were caught in weeds. Drowned dead, miss!"

"Do stop saying that!" Lucy begged. "Esther, is this true? Is the poor child really drowned?"

"Yes, Miss Lucy."

"But didn't she cry out? Didn't anyone hear her?"

"Joan was screaming, but on Sunday the mill is closed and it being such a fine day, many folk were from home."

"Isn't it terrible!" Cook who enjoyed nothing more than a tragedy was weeping lustily. "Shall I give the little lass a drop of summat, for the shock?"

"Yes, indeed, and have something yourself." Lucy turned to Esther. "If you wait a moment to catch your breath I'll drive you and Joan back to the Rowes."

"If you please, miss, I only came to fetch my things," Esther said.

"Yes, of course. You must stay over and help them. Charles!" Lucy turned as her cousin, glass in hand, lounged in. "Charles, they're saying that Mary Rowe has been drowned. I have to go down there to see what can be done."

"Drowned! Poor lass!" Charles's face stiffened. "What happened?"

"They were fishing down by the river, she and Joan," Esther said in her gently respectful manner. "Mary slipped into the deep water and was caught by the weeds. Joan ran for help and some of the men pulled Mary out, but she was dead."

"Good God!" He stared after Cook and Jessie who were ushering Joan into the kitchen.

"It is all right for me to drive them back, isn't it? And the doctor will have to be called," Lucy said.

"I'll ride over to Otley. Doctor Ferguson's staying there with his sister for a few days."

Charles patted her on the shoulder, thrust the brandy into her hand and hastened to the back quarters.

"If you please, miss, Joan and I can walk back," Esther said.

"Nonsense! It's no trouble."

"It would be better if you stayed here, miss," Esther said stolidly.

"I wasn't going to intrude," Lucy said, beginning to feel hurt.

"I know, miss, but it's best you don't. Mrs Rowe is very hysterical," Esther said. "Don't be angry, but she keeps saying you caused it."

"Caused what? Esther, what are you talking about?"

"You said that Mrs Rowe ought to keep her girls at home," Esther said. "And just after you left the house, Joan ran up to tell us Mary had been pulled out of the river."

"But that's — I never heard of anything so silly in my life." Lucy, in her agitation,

189

walked back into the parlour.

"Yes, Miss Lucy, but it's best you stay at home," Esther said. "May I get my things now?"

"Yes, yes, of course. Will you tell Saul — tell him that I would like to see him when it's convenient?"

"See Saul, Miss Lucy?"

"On a matter of business. That's all."

Deeply disturbed, Lucy went up the main stairs. The task of breaking the bad news to her aunt lay ahead, and she was well aware that would entail long explanations, tears, and copious draughts of tea.

The death of a child was no uncommon occurrence in the Hollow, but Mary Rowe had survived the perilous years of infancy, and to be drowned in a river along which she had played all her life was regarded as something out of the common run. Lucy, keeping close to the house, was aware of an undercurrent among the servants. It seemed to her that when she entered the kitchen they stopped talking or quickly changed the subject.

Charles had come back from the inquest with the information that the verdict had been one of accident. The coroner had expressed sympathy with Mrs Rowe, and those who had attended the inquest had

190

trickled back to their homes. Mary's funeral had been a private one and nobody from the Holden family had gone, though Cook had attended and was ready to talk about it to Jessie.

"Anna Rowe looked poorly. Thin as a drain she is and her face all drawn. Saul was carrying the coffin — him and the two lads. Esther had to stay back to care for young Annie and Emma's babe."

She had broken off as Lucy came in and begun to scold the younger maid for not ironing the sheets thoroughly.

Lucy had waited, with as much patience as she could muster, for Saul to come. With the inquest and the funeral over it was only his stubborness that kept him away.

"And I," said Lucy fiercely to her reflection in the glass, "will not run after him, begging!"

But there were long evenings when she sat at her open window, listening to the sound of the beautiful treacherous river, watching twilight creep down to embrace the valley.

"You look peaked, my dear," Aunt Trinity remarked. "I know that I seldom stir myself, but you are young and a little air would do you no harm. The evenings will be drawing in soon, and then the frosts will come, and you will be stuck here with no remedy."

She gazed with vague apprehension at her niece. The child had always been pale but now she looked ghostly, and she had lost weight which she could ill afford to do.

Nothing, Trinity thought, had gone right since poor Edward had died of the fever. She had never cared very much for Sarah Lumley nor understood how Charles could prefer Holden Hall to Ladymoon Manor, but she had never spoken a word against the engagement. And then Emma Rowe had spoiled everything with her announcement. Trinity, who had observed her son's interest in the maid with commendable tolerance, felt extremely irritated by his thoughtless conduct, and even more irritated by his refusal to admit responsibility. Lucy said the babe was a typical Holden. It was too provoking that she was denied the pleasure of spoiling her first grandchild. And Tabitha was such a sweet name.

"I'll take a turn in the garden," Lucy said, making her aunt jump slightly for Trinity had quite forgotten her previous remark.

August was drifting into September in a lazy, contended way. In the orchard apples and pears hung heavy from the crowded branches, and the wind was heather scented.

Lucy walked slowly across the lawn, past the profusion of roses and the herb garden with its border of coloured shells. The high hedge was pregnant with meadowsweet and plump blackberries sparkled on the briars that twined about the gate.

She opened it and stood still, her eyes riveted upon the tall figure who stood on the river bank below.

"Saul? Oh, Saul, I am so very pleased to see you!" She ran lightly down the slope, her small face glowing.

"Good-day, Lucy." He half-turned, his eyes still sombre, and bowed.

"Was this — did it happen here, so close to the house?" She stared down uneasily into the deep rushing water,

"Further down," he said. "Nobody could have heard anything."

"It was an accident," Lucy said, "Nobody wished such a dreadful thing to happen."

"No. It was an accident," Saul said.

"But your mother said — "

"My mother is a sick woman. She often speaks without thought. I take no notice of local gossip."

"So there is gossip?" She caught him up on the word.

"I told you I pay no heed to it."

"Yes, I heard you." She raised her chin and said, a slight quiver in her voice. "I asked you to come and see me. Did Esther give you the message?"

"Yes, she told me."

"Then why didn't you come? The inquest and the funeral are over now, so why didn't you come?"

"I've been standing here this past half-hour," he said, "trying to decide whether or not to come up to the house. I was remembering that night you came down to show me your balldress."

"I still have it," she interrupted. "I've not worn it since."

"That was a strange night," he mused. "You and me by the river."

"And Esther rising up like a ghost from the reeds. I'm sure it was Esther who saw us, though she and I have never spoken of it."

"I desired you that night," Saul said. "I had such a fierce desire for you."

"And I for you." She looked at him with a touch of fear. "We are talking as if we are all in the past, as if we had grown old and were in danger of forgetting. But I still feel as I did, and mean what I meant then. It's still like that for you, isn't it?"

He was silent, looking at her, and in panic she seized his arm, crying. "Isn't it, Saul? Isn't it?"

"It's too late," he said at last.

"Too late? Because of Emma and the

baby? Because Charles will not admit the babe is his?" she demanded.

"That was part of it," he said slowly. "If Emma is not good enough to wed Mr Charles, then how could you and I ever hope to be married?"

"I am not my cousin, and you are not your sister. We are two different people, Saul. We have our lives to lead."

"Your cousin would not give his consent."

"My aunt is my legal guardian, not Charles. She will easily be persuaded. She thinks well of the Rowes, of all your family, and my cousin's conduct has grieved her. Our marriage might help to heal the breach."

"That's a romantic tale for children."

"It's a tale we could make true," she said eagerly. "Saul, I haven't any money. I haven't any dowry at all. You'd be making no bargain."

"I never had that in mind," he said.

"I know, I know. I'm trying to make you understand how it could be, if you could only put aside your pride."

"If a man puts aside his pride he may as well stop being a man."

"And love?" she questioned. "Oh, Saul, doesn't love count for anything?"

"It was like a dream," he said. "You and I riding together over to Romany Crag, you and I on the moors above Clutterhouses. A beautiful dream, and none of it real. We have to wake up."

"Wake up? But I am awake, Saul. I'm truly awake. We can be married, as soon as you please. As soon as you please!"

"It's not possible," he said, and the gentleness of his voice frightened her more than anger would have done.

"Of course it's possible," she said. "Anything is possible if you only want it badly enough. You do care for me? Oh, it isn't for a lady to say, but you're forcing me to say it."

"I was coming to see you," he said, "because I wanted to tell you before you heard it elsewhere."

"Heard what? Saul, what is it?"

"I'm wed," he said hoarsely. "I married Esther Evans over at Otley this afternoon."

"It's not true," she said blankly. "It's not true."

"It was very quiet, because of my mother's bad health and Mary's death so recently.

"Married Esther? But you don't love her. You *cannot*!"

"Not as I feel for you," Saul said. "But she's a gentle girl, and she's made herself so useful about the house."

"Is that a reason to wed her? Because she's useful about the house?"

"She suits me and I need a wife."

"Don't I suit you?" she asked. "Didn't you stop to think that I might need a husband?"

"It was for your sake — " he began, but she cut him short, bewildered anger rising in her.

"I'll never understand how you can marry one woman for the sake of another!"

"If we were to marry," he said, "how and where would we live? At Ladymoon Manor with the man who shamed my sister and refuses to admit it? At my mother's house when she swears you ill-wished my father and sister to death?"

"Your father died of a stroke! What had I to do with that?"

"Jenny Rathbone swears you cursed him a short while before, when he was making her two lads go into work."

"And you believed that!"

"Of course not. It's foolish gossip and I pay it no mind, but my mother and Emma believe it."

"We'd live in our own house," Lucy said. "Not at Ladymoon, or with your mother, but in our own place. I've been poor, Saul. When I was a child we lived in two rooms, my father and I. We used to pawn things in order to buy food."

"There's no pawnshop here-abouts and if there were I'd not have my wife going to it."

"I wasn't being literal," she said wearily. "We could be comfortable in a small house. That's all I'm trying to say."

"Had I married you how long do you think I'd have been kept as an overseer?" Saul demanded. "I'm overyoung for the job as it is. And there's another thing. Bad enough to work for a man who's shamed one's sister. Much worse if that man is your own wife's cousin. I thought it out, over and over, and I asked Esther to wed me."

"And I had no voice in it? No opinion? You gave me no thought?"

"I thought only of you and shall do to my life's end."

"Then you cheat us both," she said, "and I'll not wish you joy in your marriage."

"It's a chance I'll take," he said. "Good day, Miss Lucy."

It was impossible that he could turn away and leave her with no gesture or word of affection or regret. But he was already striding along the river bank in the direction of the mill, without pausing to turn his head.

Lucy moved nearer to the brink and stared at the rushing water. The river, like herself, was a creature of many moods, It was lively now, but beneath the white rimmed waves lay still depths, thick with weeds, crowded with fish that swam like secret thoughts below the surface of the mind.

Mary Rowe had died here, sliding under the water, held fast in the weeds, troubles ended.

"Saul is wed," Lucy told the rushing water. "He has married Esther Evans, the girl I befriended and took into the house. Isn't that a kind of joke?"

At moments of great crisis tears deserted her and her throat closed up over a lump of misery.

She stared for a moment longer at the river and then, her head high, walked swiftly up to the gate again. The manor house looked exactly as it had looked a short while before. She gazed at it in a sort of wonder, imagining how often during its centuries people must have entered it in states of bliss or unhappiness. Its very walls must be soaked in emotion, yet it retained an air of tranquillity.

Her aunt was dozing by the parlour fire. Lucy tiptoed past, unable to face the prospect of being drawn into an exchange of trivialities. In the hall she was confronted however by her cousin, and his questioning look made her heart jump a little.

"Is anything wrong? You look very white."

"I went down to the river." She evaded his hand and went through into the library. Charles had evidently just risen from his chair, a half-empty brandy glass mute testament of his presence. He seemed, however, to be completely sober, and his voice was so kind that she felt the sting of tears behind her eyes.

"What ails you, cousin? I saw you walking through the garden as if you had just learned of another death."

"I was thinking about Mary Rowe, thinking how dreadful it must be to drown."

"I was flattering myself that you might be regretting your refusal of me," he said.

"Regretting?" Her green eyes blank, she stared at him.

The first shock was wearing thin, her numb despair being stripped away to reveal the bitter grief and anger that lay below.

"The offer is still open," Charles said.

"To marry you?"

If she married Charles she would be able to live at Ladymoon Manor for the rest of her life. She could shelter within its protecting walls and seldom go down to the Hollow at all.

"We'd suit well," Charles said as he had said before.

"I think we might," she said slowly. "Aunt Trinity would be pleased and I am very fond of you."

"We could be married very quietly," but she interrupted, her voice sharpening a little. "I would prefer a larger wedding, if you don't object. With a reception at York, and a second reception here for all the village."

"As you choose." He concealed his surprise. "Mother will be delighted for she's been in low spirits these past months."

"I don't want a long betrothal." she said. "I'd like to be wed before Christmas."

"Next month if you wish." He was moving towards her, his expression a mixture of affection and amusement. She closed her eyes, enduring the pressure of his lips. Perhaps 'endurance', she thought in confusion, was the wrong word. The embrace, at any other time, might have been pleasing.

"Shall we wake Aunt Trinity?" she asked, opening her eyes and withdrawing a little.

"Yes, of course." He watched her leave the room and a slight bewilderment creased his brow. There seemed to be something different about Lucy this afternoon and he was not certain if he understood what it was.

7

"Time rushes by so quickly," Trinity said, "that one scarcely realises today is come before it is tomorrow!"

Lucy, glancing up from the purse she was tatting, nodded sympathetically. She was well aware, however, that her aunt required no answer but would chat on happily until sleep or the desire for food overcame her.

"It seems incredible," she was saying now, "that so much has happened. Poor Edward gone, and Tabitha already sitting up, and you married to Charles, and Saul Rowe married to Esther."

Her pretty voice trailed into vagueness, but the glance she shot at her niece was a sharp one. Had anyone troubled to enquire of her, she would have sworn that Lucy and Saul Rowe had enjoyed some kind of romantic understanding the previous summer. The girl had contained such joy in her face, and then she had announced she was going to be married to Charles and though she had smiled and blushed and said all the correct things, her aunt had looked in vain for any trace of joy.

202

Certainly it had been a very grand wedding with Lucy looking beautiful in creamy satin flounced with blue ribbon knots. Trinity had suggested that silver ribbon would give a more delicate effect, but Lucy had said sharply that she preferred the blue.

They had stayed in York for the wedding and for the official reception at which Trinity had met nearly everybody she knew and a great many she didn't. Daniel Lumley hadn't come, but he'd sent a handsome bracelet of diamonds set in gold.

It was years since she'd bothered to go into York, and it had been part sweetness, part sorrow to see again the places so familiar to her and Matthew. She had visited his grave and lingered to look at others. Her aunt, Tamar Makin, and Tamar's father, Sir Petroc Makin and right back to Sir Joshua Makin and his 'helpmeet'. Yoni, who'd lived at Ladymoon Manor in the early seventeenth century. Generations of men and women who had lived in the old house and taken to their graves the secrets of their joys and sorrows.

And before the Makins there had been the Scardales of whom she had heard only vague tales, of their having been a Catholic family in the time of the persecutions of Queen Elizabeth, of one of the Scardales having been a witch or a lunatic, or possibly both.

Those must have been exciting times, she thought. These days there was no colour in life, only the constant threat of French invasion, the ceaseless battle to raise profits, talk of lay offs and new looms.

There had been no wedding trip, but there had been a second reception at the mill, an open air supper at which toasts to the bride and groom had been drunk and nobody had mentioned the previous supper when Sarah Lumley had stood among them with a diamond on her finger.

Saul Rowe had been there with Esther at his side, but he'd left early, and when the Holden carriage passed the Rowe house Emma, either by accident or design, was standing at the door with the baby in her arms.

There had been a defiant tilt to her chin and Trinity had felt a pang of pity for the girl, she had not ventured to say anything to Charles or to Lucy.

"I think I'll drive down to the Hollow and meet Charles," Lucy said, putting aside her work.

"Yes, do." Trinity's face brightened as she spoke. Any sign of affection between her son and her niece was welcomed by her. Not that they ever quarrelled, she consoled herself, but they treated each other with cool friendliness in which there was no trace of passion.

Lucy kissed her cheek and went out into the hall, taking her cloak and bonnet from the stand.

While she was waiting for the pony and trap to be hitched she occupied herself with putting on her outdoor things, fluffing out her curls from under the brim of her straw bonnet, tying a bright ribbon over the crown to hold it fast on her head. She spent a lot of time making herself look pretty these days, sometimes changing her dress two or three times a day, and driving out on the moor with no clear idea of where she intended to go.

She seldom went down to the Hollow or to the mill, for she was conscious of the glances cast at her by the village women. Anna Rowe had died of the pain in her side the previous January and since then there had been whispers and sidelong glances whenever Lucy appeared. The glances were only sidelong and the whispers were low, but they shivered through her.

Yet, of late, she had taken to driving down to the mill in the same way as some people were compelled to scratch a sore even though the temporary relief ended in its bleeding afresh.

At the Rowe house she slowed the trap and glanced sideways at the open door. Emma was not there, but she was back at the mill again, working part time at the spinning, while Esther cared for the babe. It was Esther however whom she wished, and dreaded, to see. Esther, with her shy, gentle look and slight figure swollen now in the last months of pregnancy. That was the sore that bled anew every time it was scratched.

Esther was not at the door and there was no glimpse of her at any of the windows. Lucy urged the horse past and trotted briskly down the street, avoiding the deep ruts which disfigured its surface. Winter and the heavy rains of spring had further dilapidated the houses. Roofs and windowledges sagged and gaped under the bright sky, and a general air of poverty and hopelessness clung to the whole scene.

To her surprise, although it was only just past four, many of the looms stood idle and a group of men and women were arguing and gesticulating in the mill yard. They moved aside as she drove in, the men touching their forelocks briefly, and then returned to their excited chatter.

"Charles, what is it? What has happened?" She ran up the narrow staircase into the counting house. Saul was with him and both men frowned at her entrance as if feminine curiosity was the last thing they desired.

"They've just heard there are new looms coming," Saul said. His face was grim, his voice hostile.

"New looms? There must be some mistake," Lucy began. "Charles has not ordered any."

"I've ordered four," Charles said briefly.

"But you said you'd not do such a thing!" she exclaimed.

"I said I'd hold off for as long as possible, but I cannot hold off my own need," Charles said irritably. "Demand for cloth is rising and we cannot meet that demand at our present rate of production."

"Why cannot we buy more of the old looms?" she demanded.

"And employ more labour to whittle more of my profits? That's not long term wisdom."

"But you will have to dismiss men, won't you?"

"I'll have to lay off some, I agree."

"Thirty two," Saul said. "Thirty two men out of a hundred, Mr Charles."

"There'll be more work for the spinners."

"Spinners are not weavers. You'll not get a skilled weaver to sit and spin with the women."

"Then I'll employ more women."

"And pay less to them. What are their menfolk to do?"

"Every man laid off," said Charles patiently, "will receive five pounds compensation and a good reference, provided he's worked at the looms for a minimum period of three years."

"Which cuts out twelve of the lads at once. Are they to starve?"

"There are plans for increased transport facilities. A road-building scheme is being mooted at York."

"You'll not get a skilled weaver to start breaking stones," Saul warned. "And I doubt if any road building scheme will pass within ten miles of the Hollow,"

"By God, but I took you for an intelligent man!" Charles exclaimed. "Times are changing and we must change with them or be driven under. If I don't install the new looms now we'll be forced out of business by the larger mills within six months, and then you'll all be out of work because I shall be bankrupt."

"If you bought ten new looms and extended the sheds that would save twenty of the men from being laid off," Saul suggested.

"I've not the capital to lay out even if I wished, and it would only stave off the evil day. Look, you can see the figures for yourself," Charles said impatiently. "To begin with I cannot obtain the raw wool I need from my own flocks. I have to buy half of it on the open market and then pay carriage to have it brought here. My annual wages bill for the spinning is eighty-seven pounds ten. Then the stuff has to be taken to the dyeing vats at Otley, carted back and set upon the looms. And there's a further amount of one-hundred and ninety three to be paid to the weavers and piece workers. Then there's the carting to Halifax and the wool tax to be taken out of the profits. By cutting the work force by thirty two I save fifty six pounds, and that's little enough in all conscience when the new looms cost three hundred each."

"Why not buy ten looms and lay off eighty men? That would save you a hundred and forty pounds a year," Saul gibed.

"You talk as if your own livelihood were in danger," Charles said. "Between the lot of you you're pulling in nearly twenty-five shillings a week. And there's another saving I have in mind."

"Oh?" Saul regarded him with suspicion.

"The midday meal provided for the women and children — "

"Which your father began."

"Which my father began, and which cost him twenty pounds a year now costs me eighty-three. It's uneconomic and encourages them to sit around gossipping."

"Charles, you cannot deny them their dinners." Lucy, who had stood silent, began to plead. "The little ones need a good meal and time to play about in the fresh air. The hours they work are so long."

"No child under twelve works more than ten hours a day in my mill," Charles said. "And I'll employ nobody under the age of five, which is more than many can say."

"But Charles — "

"That's sufficient, my dear. You have no right to interfere," he corrected.

"Where there is injustice I'll claim that right!"

"You'd best go home, Miss Lucy," Saul said.

"To twiddle my thumbs while men pull the world apart between them, I suppose? I wondered if you were ready to come home yourself, Charles."

"With half my hands down there arguing the rights and wrongs of it! You'd best get them back to their work Saul."

"They'll want assurance that ample compensation will be paid, and further lay offs avoided before they'll settle down."

"Settle down! Good Lord, you talk as if they owned the mill instead of being employed here!" Charles said angrily.

"They want to know the ins and outs of it," Saul said.

"Then they shall!" Charles crossed to the window and tugged it open. There was a hush from below and Lucy, moving to stand behind him, could glimpse the upturned faces.

"Friends, these are hard times," Charles began.

"Tell us summat new, Master," a voice shouted back.

"Hold your noise, Will Beeston, and let me finish," Charles demanded. "To keep pace with demand and with our competitors we have to produce more and cheaper cloth. That means new looms."

"And men out of work!" another shouted.

"Thirty-two will be laid off," Charles acknowledged. "Young, unmarried men who will find it easier to get other work. They'll receive five pounds compensation if they've three years service in hand, two pounds for less. The new looms will be brought in at the beginning of the week. I've held off for as long as possible, but now I'm forced to it. I shall pay a bonus of two pounds a man to those who will volunteer to bring the looms from Halifax."

"Bring them in yourself!" Beeston called.

"There's none here will soil his hands wi' blood coin!"

"*You* are asking to be laid off," Charles said coldly.

"Do so! By next year you'll have more looms in and more of us idle," the weaver retorted, "if we don't put a stop to it now."

"Where dost tha stand, Saul Rowe?" another cried.

"Stands with the master," came a mocking comment, "for wasn't it the master who lay with his sister and put a bastard in the family?"

"Keep thy dirty talk to thysen!" One of Saul's dark-browed younger brothers lunged into the crowd.

The other, Jacob, shouted, "Come down and stand with us, brother!"

"Hush your noise or you'll be laid off too," Emma hissed.

Lucy could see her clearly, black hair tumbling over her shoulders, arms akimbo on the hips of her red skirt.

"You'd best go back to the manor," Charles said, glancing at his wife. "Saul, see her to the trap."

She opened her mouth to argue but Saul, his hand on her shoulder was ushering her to the door. As the darkness of the staircase hid them from the upper room his hand slid

212

to her own, grasping it firmly.

"How do you stand?" she whispered urgently.

"Where I always did, lass, God help me!" he muttered, his fingers pressing her own and then releasing her as they came out into the yard.

"You'll not stand with the masters against your own, will you?" Jacob demanded, coming forward.

"I'll do what's right and proper," Saul answered, "and you'd do best to get back to work. I cannot speak up for you while you idle here."

He was helping Lucy up to the driving seat and the touch of his hand still burned her flesh. She gathered up the reins, glanced to where Charles still stood at the window, and drove out of the yard.

Her sympathy lay with the weavers, for she knew them to be deeply concerned with the threat to their livelihoods but she could not deny Charles her pity either. He was extremely worried about falling profits and rising prices, and she knew that he spent long hours poring over the account books night after night. As for Saul, she dare not think about him too much for his was a suffering she shared in full measure.

Charles came home late, when supper

was half over. He seemed preoccupied and answered absently when she spoke to him, but later, when she went into the library to find a book that would while away the remaining hours of the evening, he looked up from the documents spread across the table and said abruptly,

"Sit down, Lucy. I've something to say."

"About my coming to the mill? I wouldn't have done so had I known there was any trouble."

"It's been simmering for months," he said gloomily. "Well I told them the truth. If the new looms are not installed we will be bankrupt within a couple of years, and everyone will be laid off. I think I finally got Saul to see the sense of it, but there are trouble-makers among the others. Beeston's mouth is bigger than his brains at the best of times."

"And the looms?"

"Will be brought in, under guard, if necessary. I'll not be dictated to," Charles said grimly.

"Will there really be trouble?" She gazed up at him anxiously.

"I'm hoping not, but these are difficult times. I shall be going to Halifax in the morning and bringing the looms back tomorrow night."

"But you said — "

"I know what I said, but if we get the looms installed before they're expected to arrive, there's less risk of trouble."

"Won't they smash them when they get them in the weaving sheds?"

"And throw even more out of work? They're not so foolish. No, judging from what's happened at other mills, once they're installed the rest of the malcontents accept the inevitable. But I am not happy to be away at this juncture, leaving you and mother here."

"Then there will be trouble?"

"I hope not, but one has to be wary." He tapped a pen against the edges of the table in an irritating series of jerks. "I think it might be wise if you and mother went to York for a few days."

"That's ridiculous!" Lucy exclaimed. "What possible harm could come to us?"

"Probably none, but I'd not wish mother to be alarmed."

"She will be exceedingly alarmed if you pack her off to York without notice," Lucy pointed out. "You know she requires weeks of preparation before she can make ready to go anywhere."

"I'd feel happier if she were out of it," he frowned. "But it's likely I'll be back with the looms before they realise I've gone. But it would be wise for you to stay close to the house until I'm back."

"Yes, of course." Pleased at having gained her point Lucy nodded obediently. "Who is going with you?"

"Nobody."

"But how will you get back the looms?" she enquired.

"The bonus I offered found no volunteers." He threw the pen down to the table. "I'll hire men in Halifax. There are Irish there working on the new road who'll be glad of the opportunity to pick up some extra money."

"Does Saul know?"

"I've not told him yet. Oh, I'll not insult him by doubting his loyalty, but he's in a difficult position. His personal dislike of me — "

"Would never influence his judgement," Lucy said.

"I hope your opinion of him is correct. His own of me is grossly in error."

It was the first time he had referred to Emma's claim that he was the father of her child. Staring at him Lucy was shaken by doubt. He spoke so firmly and had remained so adamant in his refusal to acknowledge responsibility that the possibility of his being innocent crossed her mind. Yet there was no doubt that Tabitha was a Holden.

"You'd better say as little as possible to Mother then if you're determined to stay here," Charles said. "Goodnight, my dear."

He kissed her cheek with affection, just as he kissed her after he had made love to her. Her own pleasure in those shared moments of intimacy never went beyond the physical, but Charles never seemed to notice.

He had gone when she woke in the morning and Aunt Trinity was full of complaints at the breakfast table.

"I cannot understand how he could have grown up so thoughtless after being so carefully reared, but manners are not what they were! Just look at yourself, my dear! Had I slouched over my food in such a fashion my Aunt Tamar would have been most annoyed."

"I'm sorry, aunt." Lucy sat up straight.

"Neither was I allowed to crumble my bread and flick it about my plate," Trinity said. "I am most put out by all this coming and going. *And* it looks like rain."

Her normally sweet temper was unusually ruffled. Lucy wondered if any hint of the new looms coming had reached her ears.

After breakfast Aunt Trinity went into the back quarters, having evidently decided on one of her periodic forays into the running of the household. At least she could work off her ill humour on the pots and pans, Lucy thought, excusing herself.

It did indeed look like rain and the day stretched ahead. If she had married Saul — but she closed her mind firmly against the wistful thought.

By now Charles ought to be nearing Halifax. It would take him the rest of the day to hire a transport gang, and then the looms would be dragged on their frames over the high tracks that snaked across the moors.

She went into the parlour and stared moodily through the window. It would have been better if she could have gone with Charles, but a wife was expected to stay close to the house.

At the end of the garden a figure appeared briefly and waved. She was alert in a moment, pleasure and apprehension mingling in her. For the first time Saul had come into the grounds of Ladymoon with the intention of seeking her.

She hurried to meet him, neglecting to pause for a cloak or outdoor shoes. He stood outside the gate on the high bank above the river and his face was grave.

"What is it? What ails you?" She looked up at him anxiously.

"Trouble," he said briefly.

"At the mill?"

"Has Mr Charles gone for the looms?" he demanded.

"Didn't he tell you then?"

Saul shook his head.

"He didn't turn up at the mill this morning. I guessed he'd set off to Halifax to bring the looms in early. Yet he leaves you here unprotected."

"You talk as if we were under siege!" she exclaimed. "As a matter of fact Charles wished me to go to York with Aunt Trinity. I saw no necessity for running off like a frightened rabbit. There's hardly likely to be murder committed because a few men are put out of work!"

"Not deliberately, but when men's passions are inflamed violence can spring up without warning. There have been millowners set upon and their families terrorized — "

"By weavers who are starving. Nobody in the Hollow is starving."

"Few are well-nourished either," he retorted. "Even men like Tom Turley — "

"Surely Tom Turley's not been laid off. His wife is too sick to work!"

"His boy, Hugh, is one of those to be replaced. That's a loss of seven shillings a week to them, and since Martha fell sick

219

their eldest lass, Alice, has had to stay home to nurse her."

"Jane and Jessie and Molly are spinners."

"Bringing in fifteen shillings a week between them. Twenty-two shillings a week to feed a family of seven with tea at fifteen shillings a pound and a loaf costing a shilling!"

"It is not my fault if prices have risen!" Lucy said indignantly.

"My dear, I know that." His voice and glance softening, he took her hand. "I know none of this is your doing, just as I know that Mr Charles is forced to bring in new looms, and the men struggle to feed their children on less money than in any previous year. It is the fault of the times."

"You talk as if a revolution were around the next corner. It couldn't possibly happen here — could it?" She looked up at him with pleading in her small face.

"I'd say it wasn't at all likely," Saul said comfortingly, "but riot is something else. Riot is possible."

"But my uncle built the mill and all the cottages down at the Hollow," Lucy said in bewilderment.

"And your husband has allowed them to go to rack and ruin. He has made no attempt to mend the roofs or replace broken windows, though he still demands regular payments of rent. There is no sanitation in any of the cottages, no arrangement for the disposal of refuse. Is it any wonder there are regular outbreaks of fever? Conditions are bad, but they will become intolerable if men are laid off and lose all hope of ever improving their lot. Most men have not the voice to express their grievances, but many of them will, as a last resort, use fist and stone to speak for them."

"You always make political speeches to me," she said sadly.

"It is safer so." He dropped her hand gently and stood back a pace.

"Would you not — not wish to know if I am happy?"

"You look well," he said briefly.

"And you — are you happy?" she whispered.

"Esther is a good wife," he said, "and she is not far off her time."

"So you no longer care for me?"

"Would I be here now if I'd stopped caring?" he asked roughly. "I came to warn you to leave Ladymoon Manor. Other houses have been attacked. You and Mrs Holden would be wise to go to York for a few days as Mr Charles advised. I can escort you myself."

"Are you going to York?"

"Mr Charles cannot hope to bring the new looms in by himself."

"He says he can hire a gang at Halifax. The looms are there, not at York."

"There are soldiers at York," Saul said. "Some of them can act as escort if I can get them over onto the Halifax road in time to meet Mr Charles on the way back."

"And who'd take care of the manor if Aunt Trinity and I went with you to York?"

"You could lock the place up," he suggested.

"So they could amuse themselves breaking down the doors, I suppose? Thank you kindly, but I'll stay here."

"If you were my wife — " he began.

"But I'm not," she interrupted. "I'm not your wife, Saul. You can't tell me what to do or order me what not to do. You threw away your opportunity."

"And you wed Charles Holden."

"He's a good husband," Lucy said defensively. "He is, Saul."

"Too good for my sister," he said wryly.

"Oh, not that again!" Her voice was weary. "Not the old tale, Saul. We neither of us know the truth of it, save that it spoiled what was between us."

"Spoiled?" He stepped towards her, taking

her face between his hands, talking quick and rough. "Nothing can spoil what is between us. Nothing can take away what we have. We are bound, you and I; have been bound since that day you climbed up into the trap with that shabby old bag clutched tight in your hands. I'll always be bound to you, and you to me, and we'll do nothing about it for the honour we bear."

He released her so abruptly that she almost fell, but someone was coming along the river bank.

"Emma? What are you doing here?" Saul went to meet her, his expression displeased.

"Idling, same as you! 'Morning, Miss Lucy." She bobbed a curtsey unsteadily.

"Have you been at the ale already, at this hour?" Saul demanded.

"I had a mug," she said. "I've a right to drink now and then if I choose. Anyway there's neither master nor overseer down at the mill, so I took an hour off — as you did."

Her eyes flashed mockingly between them.

"I had business to discuss with Miss Lucy."

"Out of sight of the house? Very wise of you, brother. That way Mrs Holden doesn't get to see anything, and neither does your wife!" She ended on a gasp of pain as Saul's hand flashed out to land a resounding slap on her cheek.

"Saul, don't!" Lucy began, and Emma whipped around, her cheek flaming, her voice snapping venom.

"You tell him, Miss Lucy! You give him his orders, for you're the master's wife now. He can never have you, can he, Miss Lucy? Mr Charles has you now, just as I once had him and — "

She had broken off, one hand flying to her mouth.

"And what?" Saul seized her arms and shook her violently. "And what? What were you going to say?"

"Nothing. Let me be!"

"Who else, Emma?" His fingers dug into her flesh, but his voice was quiet. "Were those tales true? About other lads? One other? Tabitha's father? Who *did* father Tabitha?"

"Edward!" Emma shouted in fury, wrenching herself free. "Mr Edward!"

"You're lying," Lucy said.

"It's true! Mr Charles wouldn't have aught to do with me after he got engaged to that Miss Lumley. I waited for him and begged him but he said he'd done with me. I went down to the counting house that same night thinking he'd ridden there, but it was Mr

Edward. And he was lover to me that night!"

"To blacken a dead man's name when he can no longer defend himself! Before God, I begin to wonder who fathered *you*!" Saul cried.

"It's true," Emma said, her voice and face still defiant. "It's true, Miss Lucy! Mr Edward wanted me that night. Perhaps he was already going off his head with the fever, but he wanted me. And he's Tabitha's father!"

"You told me it was Mr Charles," Saul said. He was staring at her as if she were a stranger.

"Because Mr Edward was dead and couldn't have married me! And it was Mr Charles I love anyway."

"And planned to cheat with his brother's child? A fine way of showing your love!"

"He wouldn't marry me anyway," Emma said sullenly. "He even stopped the money he'd been giving me for old times sake."

"Because you lied to him. Lied so cleverly that nobody believed him when he was telling the truth," Lucy whispered. "Oh Saul, don't you see? She ruined everything for all of us."

"You married him fast enough when Miss Lumley wouldn't have him," Emma said.

"To pretend that Edward's child belonged to Charles in the hope that he'd wed you was an evil thing to do," Saul said.

"No worse than to wed one lass when you lusted after another," Emma retorted slyly. "And I don't come sneaking around when your back's turned to make up to the master!"

She turned at that and flounced off, pulling her shawl over her head.

"She followed me here, I suppose." He spoke almost to himself, gazing after her.

"Will she tell Esther?" Lucy asked.

"If she drinks any more, but with luck she'll drift back to the mill and get on with her work. Anyway, Esther is no fool. She knows I don't love her. It's a matter we don't discuss. Oh, I tried once to explain to her but she didn't want to listen."

"I'm glad. I never discussed you with anybody."

"And Mr Charles was telling the truth."

"Edward was Tabitha's father."

They were talking as if they repeated words they were learning for a play, words that had nothing to do with them at all. Abruptly Lucy said, "If Emma had only told the truth Charles would at least have supported both her and the baby for Edward's sake, and you and I — would you have married me then?"

"It's too late, my little lass," he said. "There's Esther and the babe now."

"And the new looms are coming in."

"Will you go to York?"

"No, I'll stay here and wait for Charles," she said tonelessly.

"I'll be on my way then." He hesitated a moment, his face dark with unspoken thoughts, then said, "It's too late for us."

She could not bear to watch him out of sight, and the threatened rain was beginning to fall, wetting her head and face. Under the soles of her thin slippers the grass pricked. She went rapidly back to the house in time to see her aunt emerging.

Trinity's comely face bore a look of mournful satisfaction.

"I knew it would rain," she announced, "and that back pantry's in a disgusting state. I shall have to have a word with Bess."

"Charles went over to Halifax to bring in the new looms," Lucy said abruptly. "Saul thinks there may be trouble so he's gone to York to get some soldiers as escort. He wanted us to go with him."

"And you told him that the manor could not be left unprotected, I hope?"

"Yes, I did." Lucy having expected alarm, looked at the older woman in surprise.

"My dear, troubles depress but never crush

me," Trinity said. "What I cannot endure is to be left out of things. Have they gone into work today?"

"I think most of them have." Lucy briefly considered Emma's revelation and mentally postponed the telling of it.

"So we are safe until tonight, and I've little fear of anything happening then," her aunt said comfortably. "Gentlemen are apt to panic in a crisis. However I do feel it would be a wise precaution to load the guns."

"Do you know how to load them?" Lucy enquired.

"You forget I was brought up in a frontier country and didn't come to England until I was fifteen," Trinity said. "We lived in a log cabin, my dear, and we set traps, fished the river, and went hunting with rifles. I am not saying that I ever caught anything very much, but I am still capable of taking a few pot-shots at a trespasser!"

8

The clock around which the two fishes wreathed showed nine and the mellow tones of the grandmother clock in the parlour confirmed the hour. It was still raining, a fine, slanting sheet of spray that obscured vision. The wind had dropped and in the silence she could hear the splashing of the river over its winding banks. Despite the fires banked up glowingly and the shuttered windows the house was chilly. Lucy had changed into a thicker gown but she still had the impulse to shiver. A mug of hot punch would, she decided, be pleasant. Cook and Jessie had already retired to bed but Bess was still clearing away in the kitchen.

"Is all quiet, dear?" Aunt Trinity looked up as she came through the parlour.

"Quiet as the grave," Lucy said, and immediately wished she hadn't.

Aunt Trinity however rose calmly, putting her cap straight as she announced,

"In that case I think I'll go up. I am sure nothing is going to happen at all, but if there is — "

"I'll wake you at once," Lucy promised.

"Are you going to sit up? Charles cannot be back until dawn."

"Only for a little while. I shall get Bess to make me a mug of punch and then I'll go to bed too."

"I shall take one of the guns up with me. You had better do the same. Goodnight, Lucy."

Trinity kissed her niece affectionately and wandered out, carrying the rifle in a manner which suggested she had completely forgotten how to use it. Lucy, having returned the embrace went into the kitchen where Bess had just hung the damp towels over the range.

"Mull some punch for me, there's a good lass. I'm going to sit up a while," she said briskly. "Is everywhere safely locked?"

"Yes, miss." The girl hesitated, then said, "Jem and the stable lads have gone out, miss."

"Out? At this hour? Where?"

"I don't rightly know, miss. I saw them setting off when I was bolting up out back. Have they gone to meet Mr Charles?"

"I expect so. Go to bed now, Bess, and I'll finish this myself."

"Yes, miss." Bess bobbed an obedient curtsey.

Finishing the hot drink, Lucy carried the

brimming mug through to the parlour and sat down by the fire. She had opened one of the shutters and through the dark glass she could see raindrops briefly sparkle in the glow of the lamplight.

All day she had avoided thinking about what Emma had said. Now in this bright, cheerful apartment she sipped the comforting punch and thought of how it might have been had Emma told the truth. Charles would have supported the babe and Sarah Lumley would have married him, and Saul — but at the thought of Saul she was hurt by a pain that no drink could comfort.

A persistent tapping on the window-pane startled her out of a doze. She was on her feet at once, staring back at the white face pressed weirdly against the dark glass. Joan Rowe, one hand clutching a shawl round her head, was rapping with her knuckles. Lucy ran into the hall and unbolted the front door, pulling the girl within. Joan was wet and shivering, her hair hanging lankly over her thin face.

"What ails you?" Lucy kept a tight grip on the girl who wriggled uncomfortably.

"Please, Miss Lucy, I came to see Mrs Holden," Joan whimpered.

"My aunt is in bed, what is it you want?"

"'Tis Esther, miss. She's had a babe and I cannot stop the bleeding."

"A babe, but it's not due yet."

"She was took bad, miss, and the babe came quick. 'Tis a little lad."

"But why come here? Where is your sister, Emma?"

"Gone to meeting with the rest of the women."

"Meeting? What meeting?" Lucy was reaching for her cloak.

"I don't know, Miss Lucy. I was told to stay home with Esther. But I'm scared, miss, for she'll not wake up and she's bleeding bad!"

"I'll come with you." Discarding the idea of wasting time by harnessing the trap, Lucy stepped out into the rain and, still holding Joan, ran towards the stables.

"We can ride double on the mare," she said briskly. "Help me get the doors open, there's a good lass!"

"Our Emma says as how thou rides a besom," Joan gasped.

"Does she indeed! Tonight we'll ride horseback like ordinary folk," Lucy said. "Come now! Up we go!"

She had ridden bareback several times on past summer days when she and Saul had run races for a dare. Now, with rain splashing her face and the shivering Joan held fast in the circle of her arm, she urged the mare over the cobbles onto the broad track that ran over the curve of the moor to the top of the street.

The Rowe house was lit only dimly by a guttering lamp, and the door was half-open. Lucy pushed it wider and picked up the lamp, holding it high to illumine the room.

"She's through here, miss. It came too fast to get her above stairs," Joan, in whom excitement seemed to have overcome apprehension, darted ahead to pull open an inner door.

The stink of blood and urine made Lucy retch. She went further into the apartment, her eyes moving to the girl who lay still on the couch amid a heap of bloodstained sheets. Between her legs something mewed and wriggled like a small kitten.

"I tied and cut the cord, miss, like Esther told me," Joan said, "but then she began to bleed, so I ran and ran but there was nobody home, so I came for Mrs Holden. She's not bleeding now, miss."

"No. No, she isn't bleeding now." Lucy spoke slowly, looking down at the grotesquely sprawled figure. Saul had made love to this girl and the result was this tiny, extraordinary ugly scrap of humanity, already groping with fists and open mouth for nourishment. She bent and picked the child up, holding it firmly for it still bore traces of the slipperiness of birth. Its head was covered with fine black down and it squinted up at her out of Saul's dark eyes.

"She's dead, isn't she?" Joan whispered at her side. "Did I do summat wrong, miss?"

"No. You've done very well. Esther was just — not strong enough to bear a child, that's all."

"But it's a bonny little lad, isn't it?" Joan said.

"Aye, a very bonny little lad," Lucy said softly. "Joan, where is Tabitha? Did Emma take her with her when she went out?"

"No, miss. Tabitha's in the cradle upstairs in the room with our Annie. They're both sleeping."

"Bring a blanket, there's a good lass," Lucy said. "We'll need to wrap the babe warm for it was born before its time."

"Esther gave it a name, miss," Joan volunteered. "She said she wanted it named Tarquin. It was a name used sometimes by travelling folk, she said."

"Tarquin, then. Wrap Tarquin warm and sit by the fire in the other room. Someone will come before morning. I'm going to find Emma."

She patted Joan on the shoulder and handed her the child.

The village street was dark and silent save for the splashing of rain in the gutters. Lucy remounted the mare and rode down towards the mill. There were no lights burning in any of the cottages, but this was not unusual for in the Hollow people retired early. She thought she heard the crying of a child behind one of the doors but the sound died away.

The gates to the mill yard were padlocked. As she stared at them old Benjamin shuffled across behind them and peered at her.

"Benjamin! It's me, Lucy Holden. Where is everybody?"

"Gone to a meeting of some sort, Mrs Lucy. Out on the moor."

"Which direction did they take?"

"Over to the Halifax road. I came to the mill, Mrs Lucy, for if there's any trouble they might make for the counting house, and with Mr Charles and Saul Rowe away someone has to look out for things. They were thinking of retiring me, you know, and getting a younger man to work as clerk. Well, I may be old but I can still fire a gun."

He was, she saw, carrying a somewhat battered musket.

"I'm sure Mr Charles will appreciate it,"

she said kindly. "I'm looking for Emma Rowe."

"Did somebody want me?" Emma's voice was faintly slurred as she strolled out of the darkness. In the dim light of the lantern her skirt glowed red and there were ribbons knotted carelessly in her tangled hair.

"Mrs Lucy's looking for thee," old Benjamin began.

"Is she now? And what does Mrs Lucy want?" Emma asked insolently.

Lucy dismounted slowly and faced the taller young woman. Rising in her was a bitter anger quite unlike her usual flashes of ill-temper.

"Esther's child is born and Esther is dead," she said levelly. "Do you understand that, you drunken bitch? While you were off supping ale, you left a child of ten to cope with two babes and a woman near her time. And when she needed help there was none near to give it. So Esther died, and when Saul finds out where you were, he'll kill you, Emma!"

"I've been busy," Emma said.

"Busy drinking your conscience under the table? Saul won't take that for an excuse!"

"Saul's over to York. He's not been here all day."

"Neither have half the millhands, I'll be

236

bound! The whole village gone off to a meeting. Such meetings are forbidden by law, as you ought to know. And there ought to be a law against women like you, women who flip up their skirts for any man, women who lie and cheat and scheme to get their own way!"

"It's not my fault." Emma's defiance was beginning to crumble. "I came back from the meeting. I didn't stay. I was on my way home."

"Get there and stay there then." Lucy flicked the ends of Emma's shawl contemptuously. "Get your clothes changed and sober up before anybody else gets back. If anything happens to that new babe, I'll get to you before Saul does, and not even your drinking mates will know you when I've done!"

Springing to the mare again, watching Emma stumble away into the darkness, Lucy felt energy flood her. Charles was on his way home with the new looms, and it was likely the millhands had gathered to smash the machines. There had been, she knew, several instances of frame breaking in other parts of the West Riding. The least she could do was to try and find Charles, to warn him of what might be. Saul might not have succeeded in obtaining help in York, and even if he had there was little chance of that help arriving in time.

She had never ridden so far by herself before, and never at night. The darkness, the slashing rain that soaked her cloak until it hung in sodden folds about her, the faint moaning of the wind as it screamed above the valley — all combined into a wildness that found its echo in her own nature.

The moon came out from behind scudding clouds and the short grass silvered briefly. The broad track ran ahead of her, dipping and rising in troughs of rippling water and patches of dark and treacherous peat. Then the darkness and the rain closed in around her again and she urged the mare on once more.

There were noises ahead of her and she shortened rein, hissing to her mount as the animal, held in mid gallop, slithered to a stop. The ground fell away into a hollow and within that hollow a crowd of people, dark, unrecognisable figures, milled and argued. Voices, distorted by rain and distance and curving landscape, filtered to her.

"Must we sit all night waiting for master t' come by?"

"He'll not come. He'll not risk bringing the frames in by himself."

"Tha talks like a fool. He'll have those

238

Irish bastards from new road wi' him!"

"I've left three bairns at home, and they'll likely wake and — "

"Hist! Someone is coming."

She had moved nearer and the moon chose that instant to blaze forth again, silhouetting her on the rim of the sloping bank.

"'Tis Miss Lucy! How in God's name came she to follow?"

"Old Benjamin'll have told her. I said we should've hushed his clack!"

She stiffened her back and rode in among them. The night had altered them, lending a sinister aspect to white faces and ragged shawls and lank hair that straggled from under the brims of low crowned hats.

"There are soldiers coming," she said, raising her voice. "Saul Rowe is bringing a detachment of soldiers to escort the new looms!"

"She's lying!" someone shouted. "Soldiers are at York."

"They are coming here, to the Halifax road. You cannot stand against rifle and musket!"

"We've muskets of our own," William Beeston roared, shouldering his way to the front. "And we're fighting for our lives, for our homes and bairns and women. We'll smash the frames and the heads of those bringing them if they try to stop us!"

"You were always a trouble-maker, Will Beeston!" Lucy flashed.

"Because I speak my mind and don't bow my head when my betters speak? I speak for my rights, Miss Lucy, and the rights of my neighbours. I'll not stand by and watch them starve."

"If you smash these they'll bring more in."

"Then we'll smash them too," Beeston declared.

"Then you'll be arrested and transported," she cried. "You cannot win! None of you can win! You'd do better to go quietly home before something dreadful happens."

"She's ill-wishing again!" shrilled a female voice. Tom Turley's wife pushed her way through the crowd. Even in the darkness it was possible to see the ravages of chronic disease in her sunken eyes and sharp-boned face as she shook her fist and called out, "Our Johnny was fit till she got the lad into the infirmary at York."

"That's not true! His leg was very bad."

"It got worse after you noted it," Martha Turley cried, "and he died, didn't he? Just like Elisha Rowe died and young Mary was drowned."

There were mutterings among the others

and she had an impression of their drawing nearer, forming a semi-circle about the mare. One or two had kindled torches and the light guttered feebly in the drenching rain.

Looking about her Lucy caught sight of Jem and called out to him, her voice sharp with anger and fear, "You're dismissed, Jem! Your work was never in danger."

"But his cousin's lads are both laid off," Beeston interrupted.

"Don't stand too close, Will," Martha called out. "Or she'll ill wish thee too. Didn't she overlook my Johnny and Elisha and Mary Rowe?"

"This is insane," Lucy said, "You are all run mad! I never overlooked anybody in my life. I wouldn't know how to do it. Please, listen to me! Don't cause any more trouble. Esther is dead of her first born because there were no woman to help, because Emma was off somewhere quaffing ale, because Joan was all alone and didn't know what to do."

She stopped aware that the faces around her had grown sharper and harder. Then from among them one of Saul's brothers shouted, "Esther was feared of Miss Lucy but wouldn't say why. Reckon we know why now, eh?"

"You're mad!" she repeated desperately.

"This is eighteen hundred and eleven, not the middle ages!"

"They had more sense then," Beeston declared. "They swam witches to test their truth."

"She came out of nowhere," Jenny Rathbone said. "I'm sorry, Miss Lucy, for tha's been good to our Mary. Real good, and I'm grateful. But 'tis true that we never saw thy beginnings."

"I was born in London, as you well know," Lucy began.

"Witches can be born in London as well as any place," Jem said. "There's queer goings on up at Ladymoon, I can tell thee."

"Then you're a damn liar!" she flamed. "So scared for your own skin that you'll run with rioters! Don't ever come back to the manor, for I'll see you're whipped off it!"

"If you ever get back yourself," William Beeston mocked and caught at the mare's bridle.

A madness had possessed them all. She glanced from face to face, seeing nothing but a blind hatred where she had once seen friendliness and respect.

"Let's have her down off that high horse!" another called.

Hands, washed clean by the rain, curved towards her. The silence was more ominous than the sound of mockery, and fear gripped her heart, squeezing it with icy fingers.

In the pause between threat and attack there came another sound, like the rhythm of phantom drummers advancing through a curtain of rain. They were frozen into immobility, arms raised, faces strained with attention.

"'Tis wagons," Beeston said and his voice was soft as a woman's. "Wagons rumbling this way."

"Is it the new frames, Will?"

"Keep your voice down, your heads too!"

"They're here. On the upper road."

The rain lifted as if someone had drawn aside the corner of a curtain. Against the dark sky, silhouetted like some frieze on an ancient vase were four wagons dragged by slowly toiling horses led by figures in mufflers and broad hats, and at their head rode a tall figure on a stallion.

Beeston's grip on the rein had slackened. Tearing it free, Lucy raised her voice in a frantic warning as she wheeled the mare about and set the animal at full gallop.

"Charles! They'll wreck the frames! Charles!" Something whistled over her head and the figure on the horse sagged and fell, one foot caught in the stirrups, dragged and crushed by the flailing hooves of the stallion as it reared and bucked.

For an instant shocked silence reigned again. Then the crowd rushed forward, cudgels and muskets raised, the women trailing skirts and shawls through wet grass, clawing at the sides of the lumbering wagons.

Lucy was riding back across the moor, tears of rage and anguish pouring down her face, her hands entwined in the wet reins. Behind her yells and shouts mingled with the splintering of wood and the clash of metal on metal. It was a nightmare that had no end and she had forgotten its beginning.

Charles was dead. Nothing could have survived that musket shot. She had glimpsed Beeston's face twisted in mocking triumph, musket still smoking in his hands. Blood lust had possessed them all and she knew, without being told, that when they'd wrecked their vengeance on the frames they'd come to Ladymoon.

She rode up the dark street to the Rowe house. Its door stood wide and Joan ran down the path, her voice shaken by sobs.

"Our Emma's come back, Miss Lucy, falling down drunk, and our Annie's woken and will not be hushed, and the new babe's crying, and I cannot tell what to do!"

Saul had gone for help thus allying himself

with the masters. She could not ride past and leave his family to face possible retribution.

"We're going to the manor," she said. "We're all going to Ladymoon. You and Annie can ride the mare, and Emma and I will carry the babes."

"Emma's drunk!" Joan cried, but Lucy ignored her and went briskly up the path.

Fire and lamp had burned low. Emma was sprawled in a chair, an expression of sleepy satisfaction on her face. Glaring, Lucy was strongly tempted to leave her where she was. But she was Saul's sister and Charles, even if he was not Tabitha's father, had used her for his own pleasure. Near at hand was a bucketful of water. Not without pleasure Lucy upended it over Emma's head, following up with several ringing slaps across the other's flushed cheeks.

Emma was struggling to rise, sneezing and spluttering, dark eyes still blurred.

"Mr Charles is killed," Lucy said loudly, "and they're on their way to murder us all. Get your babe and come with me."

Grief, intense and bitter, flashed into Emma's face. Lucy thought with sudden compassion, "Why, she really did love him!"

"Hurry! We've a mile to walk," she said curtly and bent to pick up the mewling babe.

245

He was smaller than Tabitha had been but then he'd come before his time. Unwillingly, to judge from his furious screwed-up face.

Joan, Tabitha in her arms and Annie whimpering at her skirts, came downstairs. Emma, shivering but evidently in command of herself, took her child who, despite being pressed to her wet bodice, slept on placidly. Joan, her eyes enormous in her pinched little face, was hoisting Annie up on the mare's broad back and scrambling up herself. Lucy looped the reins over her wrist, and with Tarquin held tightly in his cocoon of blanket, began to lead the horse into the darkness of the broad lane that arched round towards the manor. Behind them Emma lurched, her skirts clinging wetly, the baby girl still sleeping.

It was fortunate that mare and mistress knew the road so well, for she had no lantern and the pouring rain made the surface thick with mud. It was with the liveliest relief that Lucy beheld the outlines of the stables.

"The mare will be safe enough here," she said, motioning the girls to dismount. "Get that dry blanket, Joan, and give her a good rub with it. She'll stay quiet in her stall."

The mare trotted docilely into the hay scented comfort of the stable. As they hurried across the cobbled yard the back door was thrust open and Aunt Trinity, rifle cocked, her nightcap askew, called tremulously,

"Who is that? Lucy? Answer or I'll shoot!"

"Don't shoot for heaven's sake!" Lucy ran towards the door.

"You out of your bed, front door unlatched, stable lads slunk off to a meeting! What's happening?"

Bolting the door behind them as they filed through to the kitchen, Trinity spoke in complete bewilderment.

"The frames are smashed," Lucy said briefly.

"Smashed! But where's Charles?"

"Mr Charles is dead!" Emma said and began to wail, rocking to and fro with the child in her arms, and water running down her to drip puddles on the floor.

"Dead." Trinity echoed the word blankly.

"I fear so. The weavers have rioted. Esther's babe is born and needs to be fed. Where are the other servants?"

"I'm up, miss," Bess said brightly. "Jessie is hiding under the bed and Cook is getting dressed."

"Emma needs dry clothes, and the babes need milk."

"I've milk enough for both," Emma said.

"Ale-flavoured, no doubt." Lucy peeled off her own soaking cloak and kicked off

247

her muddied shoes.

"And where is Saul?" Trinity asked. "Not hurt or killed as well?"

"He went to bring back soldiers. If they strike out for Halifax and find the wagons they'll surely ride on here, to get ahead of the rioters. They may be on their way at this moment."

"But why should the millhands come here?" Trinity asked. "With Charles killed — dear God, I cannot take it in! With Charles killed and the frames broken, what more do they want?"

"They have been goaded into violence by Beeston and a few hotheads," Lucy said. "I couldn't leave Saul's family to be harmed."

"No, no, of course not. But where's Esther? You said this was her babe?"

"Esther died." Lucy said flatly.

"Esther dead too." Trinity's voice rose. "I don't understand any of this. I don't understand any of it."

"There's no time to explain, aunt," Lucy said. "Are the doors locked and all the windows shuttered?"

"Yes. Yes, I checked them myself."

"Bess, get some clothes for Emma and Joan and Annie. Emma, are you sober enough to feed the babes?"

"Yes, Miss Lucy."

248

"Joan, go with Bess to get yourself and Annie dried off. Cook!" Lucy turned as Cook, attired in a weird assortment of hastily donned garments, entered. "Cook, the little girls need to be fed and then put to bed. Better put them in my room. Can you fire a gun?"

"I never tried."

"You may have to learn very speedily. Aunt Trinity, we have no time to grieve now. There's still much you don't know, but we have to make ready to defend ourselves now. Will you rouse Jessie and make her help with the children?"

"Yes, of course." Trinity drew up her plump little figure. "You may rely on me to do everything within my power. Charles would have wished it so."

"Charles would be proud," Lucy said, and went rapidly through to the parlour. It would be sensible to rekindle the fire here too. She was too excited to feel cold, but the babes must be chilled to the bone in their wet shawls and blankets.

She opened the shutter a crack and listened. There was, at first, no sound except the splashing of the rain and then she heard as she had once heard in the carriage on her way back from Holden House, the steady tramping of feet, the shouting of men, a shot whining through the air.

"There's fighting down by the river." Aunt Trinity, the protesting Tarquin in her arms, stood trembling at her side.

Lucy gave her a swift hug and ran back into the hall. She could hear Annie crying in the kitchen and Bess trying to soothe her.

The prayer room was dim and cool and silent, like a shrine on a battlefield, she thought, and stepped within, her eyes moving to the golden cup. In a few moments there would be peace or conflict.

From her lips broke a cry that had in it all the pleading of her life.

"Lady of no name, bring Saul. Lady of no name, help us!"

No answer came. No moon shone from behind the dark clouds. But the cup glowed and throbbed, and the silver face was a promise of everything to come.

Epilogue

That was an eternity of a night. Lucy was to remember all her life the heart stopping terror of those hours that dragged towards dawn. In the little room she sat rigidly, gripping the cup. In the moonlight the face watched her, compassion in the slanting eyes, a faint smile on the lips. That smile said, 'No need to fear for all things pass in the fullness of time'.

Her eyelids drooped now and then and a series of disconnected scenes flashed across her mind. A wide road across which desert sand drifted filled with a procession of colourfully dressed people. Young girls with perfume cones on their heads and pleated dresses played flutes and gilded lyres. Shaven headed priests with leopard skin cloaks chanted in a liquid sing song litany. Enthroned on a litter draped with red and white the priestess of the moon held between her slender palms the golden chalice with the silver face. An immense building, its arches soaring up into a vaulted roof, was dim with clouds of incense that rose from burnished thuribles and thick with the lotus blossoms flung by the devout at the feet of the goddess. Beyond the stillness, along the avenue of spinxes, under the pylon gate, tramped marching feet and to the ears of the temple maidens came harsh commands barked in a foreign tongue.

There were men everywhere, their cloaks like blood, their breastplates shining, their banners eagle crowned. They came without hatred or pity, scattering girls and eunuchs, trampling the lotus flowers, and one, taller than the rest, seized the chalice from its place on the altar and thrust it beneath his cloak. Let Egypt beware for Caesar's legions have come, to pillage the holy shrine of Isis and steal away those things that are rightfully hers!

Lucy found herself shaping the warning in a soundless cry of terror, but the scenes had whirled into nothingness before she jerked upright in her chair, opening her eyes upon the little, dark panelled apartment. It was grey dawn beyond the round window and her limbs were cramped and chilled. The chalice on her lap weighed heavy as if virtue had gone out of it. She rose, straightening her shoulders, and put the cup back upon the table where it would catch the first rays of the sun.

The house was quiet. No doubt the

others slept. Moving softly, she let herself out through the front door and stood for a moment, breathing in the damp, breeze freshened morning air. The garden was wreathed in faint spirals of mist that rose from the river and spiders' webs were stretched like lace across the hedges.

With a small shock of realisation she thought, 'All this is mine now. There is nobody but me left to inherit Ladymoon Manor and the mill. Charles is dead and I am his widow'.

She could summon no real regret for the husband who had betrayed her. She could feel no grief for his violent end, for this was a violent age and he had carried the seeds of his own destruction.

At least the rioters had passed by the house. She hurried to the end of the garden and looked down the slope towards the bend in the river. No column of flame tinged black smoke rose above the trees, so presumably the mill had not been fired. It was so silent as if she were the only person in the world. Without forming any conscious intention she began to hurry down to the river bank, pushing aside the long trains of creeper, heedless of the chill striking up from the ground through the soles of her shoes.

The mill gates were open but soldiers

guarded them and kept a wary eye on the straggling group of weavers who sat or stood about in the yard. In the cold light of morning the men were hollow cheeked and dark eyed, their thin shoulders hunched in misery under their shabby jackets.

"Mistress Holden? We were about to send a runner up to the house to inform you the immediate danger is past." One of the red-coated officers approached her.

"Immediate?" She blinked slightly, trying to accustom herself to the altered state of affairs.

"The new frames were smashed, but we have the ringleaders already bound and on their way to York. They will hang, Mistress, make no mistake. That will quiet the rest for a while, and you can always bring in Irish labour — "

"Where is my overseer?" she interrupted. "Is Saul Rowe here?"

"In the counting house, I believe. May I offer my sympathy on the death of your husband? A terrible thing."

"Yes, thank you." She nodded curtly and went on towards the counting house, her face impassive under its crown of untidy red hair.

Saul was at the desk, his head bent over the ledgers. His coat was torn and his eyes, as he turned them upon her, were red-rimmed with fatigue.

"I had Charles's body taken to the church," he said, without preliminary greeting. "The frames are beyond repair but it might be possible to apply for compensation."

A little bubble of anger began to swell in her. He might have been hurt or lying dead as Charles lay dead. All night that fear had laid in her heart, and he spoke to her now as if nothing had ever bound them together except the labour disputes and his sister's shame.

"I expected you to come to the house," she said coldly. "I have been sitting there all night, waiting for news. For all I knew, the mill might have been razed and you yourself — " She broke off, pressing her lips together, horrified because tears stung her eyes.

"I would have come," he said, "but there were matters to attend here. The militia caught up with the rioters and we've averted the worst of the trouble for the time being, but there will be more trouble ahead and no hope of avoiding it."

"I'll buy new frames," she said tensely. "I'll look into the conditions of the weavers too. Charles neglected that."

"About Charles," he began, but she

hurried on, her voice hard, the tears still threatening.

"I'll have Charles buried, and I'll wear black for a year so as not to outrage the neighbours. I'll do all the correct things, I promise you. But when the year is up, what then? What about us?"

"You own it all now," he said, his face beginning to set into obstinate lines.

"And cannot manage it alone, I cannot manage my life alone. Not without you, Saul. Not without the love you promised me!"

"I've not the right," he muttered.

"I am speaking of love, Saul," she said passionately. "I am speaking of what has been between us all these years, though we never would admit it! I'm sorry that Esther died. I'm truly sorry because I know you were fond of her as I was of Charles. But they are both dead now. Dead, Saul! Does that mean that we have to creep into our own graves and stay there until we are truly dead? Are we going to deny our own selves?"

"I'll be up to the house later," he said, and there was a softening in his voice.

"To discuss the frames?" she asked sarcastically. "To talk of compensation?"

He took a quick step towards her and she was crushed against him, close within the protection of his arms, and his mouth sought her as if she were water and he were parched with thirst.

"We'll talk of the future," he said at last. "We'll plan our lives together. Will that suit you, Lucy lass?"

"Happen!" she said, and the first rays of the sun came through into the dusty counting house and made a glory of her hair.

Other titles in the
Ulverscroft Large Print Series:

THE GREENWAY
Jane Adams

When Cassie and her twelve-year-old cousin Suzie had taken a short cut through an ancient Norfolk pathway, Suzie had simply vanished . . . Twenty years on, Cassie is still tormented by nightmares. She returns to Norfolk, determined to solve the mystery.

FORTY YEARS
ON THE WILD FRONTIER
Carl Breihan & W. Montgomery

Noted Western historian Carl Breihan has culled from the handwritten diaries of John Montgomery, grandfather of co-author Wayne Montgomery, new facts about Wyatt Earp, Doc Holliday, Bat Masterson and other famous and infamous men and women who gained notoriety when the Western Frontier was opened up.

TAKE NOW, PAY LATER
Joanna Dessau

This fiction based on fact is the love-turning-to-hate story of Robert Carr, Earl of Somerset, and his wife, Frances.

McLEAN AT THE GOLDEN OWL
George Goodchild

Inspector McLean has resigned from Scotland Yard's CID and has opened an office in Wimpole Street. With the help of his able assistant, Tiny, he solves many crimes, including those of kidnapping, murder and poisoning.

KATE WEATHERBY
Anne Goring

Derbyshire, 1849: The Hunter family are the arrogant, powerful masters of Clough Grange. Their feuds are sparked by a generation of guilt, despair and ill-fortune. But their passions are awakened by the arrival of nineteen-year-old Kate Weatherby.

A VENETIAN RECKONING
Donna Leon

When the body of a prominent international lawyer is found in the carriage of an intercity train, Commissario Guido Brunetti begins to dig deeper into the secret lives of the once great and good.

A TASTE FOR DEATH
Peter O'Donnell

Modesty Blaise and Willie Garvin take on impossible odds in the shape of Simon Delicata, the man with a taste for death, and Swordmaster, Wenczel, in a terrifying duel. Finally, in the Sahara desert, the intrepid pair must summon every killing skill to survive.

SEVEN DAYS FROM MIDNIGHT
Rona Randall

In the Comet Theatre, London, seven people have good reason for wanting beautiful Maxine Culver out of the way. Each one has reason to fear her blackmail. But whose shadow is it that lurks in the wings, waiting to silence her once and for all?

QUEEN OF THE ELEPHANTS
Mark Shand

Mark Shand knows about the ways of elephants, but he is no match for the tiny Parbati Barua, the daughter of India's greatest expert on the Asian elephant, the late Prince of Gauripur, who taught her everything. Shand sought out Parbati to take part in a film about the plight of the wild herds today in north-east India.

THE DARKENING LEAF
Caroline Stickland

On storm-tossed Chesil Bank in 1847, the young lovers, Philobeth and Frederick, prevent wreckers mutilating the apparent corpse of a young woman. Discovering she is still alive, Frederick takes her to his grandmother's home. But the rescue is to have violent and far-reaching effects . . .

A WOMAN'S TOUCH
Emma Stirling

When Fenn went to stay on her uncle's farm in Africa, the lovely Helena Starr seemed to resent her — especially when Dr Jason Kemp agreed to Fenn helping in his bush hospital. Though it seemed Jason saw Fenn as little more than a child, her feelings for him were those of a woman.

A DEAD GIVEAWAY
Various Authors

This book offers the perfect opportunity to sample the skills of five of the finest writers of crime fiction — Clare Curzon, Gillian Linscott, Peter Lovesey, Dorothy Simpson and Margaret Yorke.

DOUBLE INDEMNITY — MURDER FOR INSURANCE
Jad Adams

This is a collection of true cases of murderers who insured their victims then killed them — or attempted to. Each tense, compelling account tells a story of cold-blooded plotting and elaborate deception.

THE PEARLS OF COROMANDEL
By Keron Bhattacharya

John Sugden, an ambitious young Oxford graduate, joins the Indian Civil Service in the early 1920s and goes to uphold the British Raj. But he falls in love with a young Hindu girl and finds his loyalties tragically divided.

WHITE HARVEST
Louis Charbonneau

Kathy McNeely, a marine biologist, sets out for Alaska to carry out important research. But when she stumbles upon an illegal ivory poaching operation that is threatening the world's walrus population, she soon realises that she will have to survive more than the harsh elements . . .

TO THE GARDEN ALONE
Eve Ebbett

Widow Frances Morley's short, happy marriage was childless, and in a succession of borders she attempts to build a substitute relationship for the husband and family she does not have. Over all hovers the shadow of the man who terrorized her childhood.

CONTRASTS
Rowan Edwards

Julia had her life beautifully planned — she was building a thriving pottery business as well as sharing her home with her friend Pippa, and having fun owning a goat. But the goat's problems brought the new local vet, Sebastian Trent, into their lives.

MY OLD MAN AND THE SEA
David and Daniel Hays

Some fathers and sons go fishing together. David and Daniel Hays decided to sail a tiny boat seventeen thousand miles to the bottom of the world and back. Together, they weave a story of travel, adventure, and difficult, sometimes terrifying, sailing.

SQUEAKY CLEAN
James Pattinson

An important attribute of a prospective candidate for the United States presidency is not to have any dirt in your background which an eager muckraker can dig up. Senator William S. Gallicauder appeared to fit the bill perfectly. But then a skeleton came rattling out of an English cupboard.

NIGHT MOVES
Alan Scholefield

It was the first case that Macrae and Silver had worked on together. Malcolm Underdown had brutally stabbed to death Edward Craig and had attempted to murder Craig's fiancée, Jane Harrison. He swore he would be back for her. Now, four years later, he has simply walked from the mental hospital. Macrae and Silver must get to him — before he gets to Jane.

GREATEST CAT STORIES
Various Authors

Each story in this collection is chosen to show the cat at its best. James Herriot relates a tale about two of his cats. Stella Whitelaw has written a very funny story about a lion. Other stories provide examples of courageous, clever and lucky cats.

THE HAND OF DEATH
Margaret Yorke

The woman had been raped and murdered. As the police pursue their relentless inquiries, decent, gentle George Fortescue, the typical man-next-door, finds himself accused. While the real killer serenely selects his third victim — and then his fourth . . .

VOW OF FIDELITY
Veronica Black

Sister Joan of the Daughters of Compassion is shocked to discover that three of her former fellow art college students have recently died violently. When another death occurs, Sister Joan realizes that she must pit her wits against a cunning and ruthless killer.

MARY'S CHILD
Irene Carr

Penniless and desperate, Chrissie struggles to support herself as the Victorian years give way to the First World War. Her childhood friends, Ted and Frank, fall hopelessly in love with her. But there is only one man Chrissie loves, and fate and one man bent on revenge are determined to prevent the match . . .

THE SWIFTEST EAGLE
Alice Dwyer-Joyce

This book moves from Scotland to Malaya — before British Raj and now — and then to war-torn Vietnam and Cambodia . . . Virginia meets Gareth casually in the Western Isles, with no inkling of the sacrifice he must make for her.

VICTORIA & ALBERT
Richard Hough

Victoria and Albert had nine children and the family became the archetype of the nineteenth century. But the relationship between the Queen and her Prince Consort was passionate and turbulent; thunderous rows threatened to tear them apart, but always reconciliation and love broke through.

BREEZE: WAIF OF THE WILD
Marie Kelly

Bernard and Marie Kelly swapped their lives in London for a remote farmhouse in Cumbria. But they were to undergo an even more drastic upheaval when a two-day-old fragile roe deer fawn arrived on their doorstep. The knowledge of how to care for her was learned through sleepless nights and anxiety-filled days.